MORTE D' EDEN

Or

TOM SAWYER MEETS THE ROLLING STONES

By

Jim Booth

BeachHouse Books

Chesterfield, Missouri, USA

Copyright

Graphics Credits:

Cover by Dr. Bud Banis. The front cover is composited from a photo of Jim Booth, Jim Craig, Doug Rorrer, and Gene Meeks courtesy of Jim Booth with text and enhancements by Dr. Bud Banis.

Publication date August, 2003
ISBN 1-888725-90-7   Regular print BeachHouse Books Edition
ISBN 1-888725-91-5 large print (16pt) MacroPrintBooks Edition
First Printing, August, 2003

Library of Congress Cataloging-in-Publication Data
Booth Jim 1952-
  Morte D'Eden or Tom Sawyer Meets the Rolling Stones/ by Jim Booth.
Chesterfield, Mo. : BeachHouse Books, 2003.
    p. cm.
1888725907 (regular print Beachhouse Books : alk. paper)
1888725915 (16 pt MacroPrintBooks Edition : alk. paper)
1. High school students--Fiction. 2.Male friendship--Fiction. 3. Teenage boys--Fiction. 4. Southern States--Social life and customs--Fiction.
PS3602.O67 M37 2003
                                        2003018219

BeachHouse Books

an Imprint of
Science & Humanities Press
63 Summit Pointe Ct
Saint Charles, MO 63301-0571
(636) 394-4950
www.beachhousebooks.com

MORTE D' EDEN

Contents

"Take me to the station and put me on a train,
I got no expectations, to pass through here again."
Mick Jagger, Keith Richards

"Life is just one damn thing after another."
Mark Twain

"We are but a moment's sunlight/ fading in the grass…"
Dino Danelli

"We all shine on--like the moon, and the stars, and the sun."
John Lennon

"And the days darken round me, and the years,
Among new men, strange faces, other minds."
Alfred, Lord Tennyson

CHARLIE AND GLENDA

"Ailleurs tous vos regards, ailleurs toutes vos armes,
Aimez ce que jamais on ne verra deux fois."

Alfred De Vigny

To be perfectly honest, I'd gotten myself into a state. When I get the blues, I tend to wallow in my despair until I'm impossible for anyone to bear. It had all started about a week before with a letter from Paula telling me we were through. It went like this:

Dear Charlie,

Rather than lead you on, I'll be straightforward. I don't think I can see you anymore. You see there's this boy Ron that I've been dating lately on the weekends you haven't come down. I know I haven't told you about him, but when I started seeing him he was only someone to go out with, not someone to love. But I do love him now, and he's asked me to go steady, so I'm sending back your class ring. If you would, please send mine in this box. I know this seems heartless and cruel, but telling you on the phone seemed even worse, and if I tried to tell you in person, things might turn out so that I'd stay with you a short while out of pity, and I know you don't want that. I'm going to keep your letters, though. They're witty and charming, and besides, if you become a famous writer someday, they'll be worth plenty. (Ha! Ha!)

I'd never sell them, though. They and you would always mean too much to me. Thank you for everything, Charlie. I'll always have a warm place in my heart for you. It's nice to know you've been loved. With you I've always known that. Try to think of me sometimes if it's not too much of a strain. I know I'll think of you often.

Love and friendship,

Paula

I stood out beside the mailbox, out next to the highway, in mortal peril from the rednecks that raced up and down the highway at all hours in their souped up Fords and read that letter. As I read I just felt more and more hollow inside, as if someone was reaching down inside me somehow and pulling out my heart. I sat down with my feet in the side-ditch and bent my head over and cried.

Finally I heard my mother call. "Charlie, what's taking so long out there? Your daddy's expecting *his Sports Afield.*"

I pulled my shirttail out of my pants and wiped my face. I took the rest of the mail in, threw it on the end table in the den, and went into my room before my mother could see how upset I was. I closed the door behind me as I went in. For a while I lay on my bed and reread the letter again and again. Then I got up, put the Beatles' *White Album* on the stereo, and fell back on my bed to study the squares on the ceiling.

For those who tuned in late, some background is due, I guess. I met Paula at Myrtle Beach. We lay on that beach in the daytime and walked up and down it at night. I wouldn't have minded reversing that procedure, but Paula said no, that wouldn't do, and I said okay because I loved her.

She was the kind of girl who would yell to horses. What I mean is, she lived in a suburb of Charlotte, and when I went to see her every other weekend, one way that we got away from her mother, who hated my guts, was to go for long drives in the country. One day in late summer we were riding by a pasture and there were two horses standing by the fence and I threw up my hand and yelled, "Hello, horses!" I looked over at Paula and she was looking at me like I was a new bicycle and she was eight years old and it was Christmas morning. When we drove down that same road on our way back to her house, we again passed that meadow and only one horse was there. She leaned out her window and yelled, "Hello, Charlie--horse!" Then she turned to me and grinned like a kid.

I was lying on my bed getting more and more maudlin when my mother opened my door and said softly, "Telephone, Charlie. It's Teddy."

I knew if I told my mother I didn't want to talk to him she'd realize that something was wrong and try to give me motherly sympathy which would only make matters worse. I wiped my face on the bedspread, got up, turned my stereo down, then went to the living room to answer the phone so my mother couldn't see my face and know I'd been crying.

When Teddy came on the phone, he wanted to tell me about his date with Karen Breeze, a girl who was a member of a crowd we called the "drill team" for an obvious reason. I didn't want to hear it, but it was plain from the outset that Teddy was going to tell me anyway, so I just stood there and listened without offering any comment. When he finished his harangue and asked, "What do you think about that, Charlie?" I just said, "I'll see you later, Teddy," and hung up the receiver gently.

Monday at school Teddy and Ralph wanted to tell me about a double date they'd had with two members of the "drill team." I avoided them as long as I could, but I knew that come 5th period study hall, I'd be forced to listen. As luck would have it, however, it was my turn for a library pass. Usually I turned them down so that Teddy, Ralph, and I could sit around and tell dirty jokes or exaggerate about what we'd done with some girl or other, but I just wasn't up to a stag session. So when Miss Harrold offered me a pass to the library, I took it.

"Hey, where are you going?" asked Ralph as I came back to my seat to get my books.

"To the library. I got an English paper due and I really need to look up some stuff." I picked up my things.

"Don't you want to hear about last night and Karen and Lisa?" Teddy leered good-naturedly.

"Aw, you all can tell me that stuff later when we're riding around or something. I really do have to get this work done."

"Well, hell, be that way, then," Ralph growled. I knew he wasn't really mad, though, so I waved good bye as I went out of the room. When I got down to the library halfway down the hall, I took my pass to the main desk then went over to a table in the corner that I liked to sit at because it afforded me the protection of being able to talk without the librarian or a teacher sneaking up behind me. It also afforded an uninterrupted view of all the girls on one side of the room. From there I could sit and try to look up girls' dresses.

On this day, however, I didn't feel like doing that, even though Glenda Faire, a pretty cheerleader with great legs and revealing sitting habits sat only one table away in a provocative pose. I put my books down on my table and went over to a shelf and began looking for books. I could feel Glenda watching me as I moved along the shelves looking for the English literature section. I could still sense her gaze even while I was skimming in a book about John Keats. Finally, I couldn't stand any more so I looked up and gave her my best "I'd like to get in your britches" look. She blushed, but she didn't look away. I was surprised, so, almost without realizing what I was doing I walked slowly over to her table. "Hi, Glenda," I whispered.

"Hello, Charlie," she said. "Would you like to sit here with me?"

"Sure," I said automatically. I thought to myself, *Boy, you sure don't need this*. But then I thought, *What difference could it make*? I sat down across from her. She had a pile of books spread out in front of her. She was working on her paper for Mrs. Raker's English class, too.

I looked at her for a couple of uneasy minutes while she tried to work. She looked up and said, "Don't you want to go get your books and bring them over here?" She smiled a beautiful, radiant smile. I looked over at my books to make myself stop lapping up that smile. I knew if I didn't go get them right away that some wise guy would steal them and jam them in a commode in the boys' restroom or something like that. Nothing personal against me, just one of those things high school guys find hilarious. I went over and got my books, hesitating before I went back. *What can she want? We've been in the same English class for two years and hardly ever talked.* I went back and sat down beside her, hoping I wouldn't stare at her that way. I was trying to think of something clever to say to win her approval. *Like every other stupid guy in this school.*

"What are you writing about?" Glenda asked, interrupting my mind games. I looked at her stupidly for a moment, then it occurred to me to answer. "Oh. John Keats. That poem about the knight. 'La Belle Dame sans Merci.'"

"Oh, I like his poems. I'm writing about Tennyson. You know *Idylls of the King*. I'm writing on 'Tears, Idle Tears.' It's so very sad." She paused and traced her finger across a book title. "But I guess you know all about this kind of stuff, don't you? You always write poems for the literary magazine and all. I guess I'm boring you." She looked at me shyly out of huge brown eyes.

"Uh, no, Glenda, no. You're right. That's a sad poem. Real sad." I looked at her distractedly. *Why don't you calm down?* I thought.

"Charlie?"

"Huh?" I tried to pay attention to what she was saying.

"May I ask you something?"

"Uh, sure. Anything."

"Are you upset about something?" She looked down. "I'm sorry. It's none of my business." She looked up again with those gorgeous cow eyes.

I took a deep breath and let it go. "Hey," I said, reaching over and putting my hand on hers, "it's okay. Yeah, I guess I am kind of down. It's really nice of you to notice." She turned her hand and took mine. She smiled self-consciously. I grinned like a fool. Then I thought of Teddy and Ralph. *If they could see me now they'd be nudging each other and giving each other knowing looks.* I stopped smiling. About that time I realized that Mrs. Ralston, the librarian, had slipped up behind us. *We should've moved to my table.* Glenda realized she was there in the next instant and pulled her hand away, sticking it under the table.

Mrs. Ralston walked slowly around the table so that she could face us. She leaned over toward us, resting her hands on the table. I patted my hand on Glenda's book and waited for the sarcasm to start.

"If you two love birds don't mind," she said loudly enough for half the library to hear, "you can go back to your study halls and carry on your little romance on your own time, not school time."

Glenda kept her head down, but began putting her books together. I got up slowly, gave Mrs. Ralston a look of pure disgust, and stacked my books. Glenda packed up her things. "Hey, wait for me," I whispered as loudly as I could. I followed Glenda across the library to the main desk. We checked out our books, got our passes, and turned to leave. Mrs. Ralston called out to us, "Make sure all the books you take from this library are properly checked out."

The boys guffawed and the girls twittered behind their books and magazines. The camel's back was broken, as far as I was concerned. "Where's your locker?" I asked Glenda as I opened the library door for her.

"Around the corner at the end of this hall."

"Wait for me there."

I was plotting revenge and she guessed it.

"Don't do anything crazy, Charlie," she pleaded.

"Hey, not me," I said, smiling. "Go on ahead." I shooed her out. She walked up the hall, occasionally glancing back.

As she reached the corner, I turned and yelled into the library, "Shove it, Bitch!" I slammed the library door as hard as I could and ran like hell for the end of the hall.

I came sliding around the corner, and Glenda practically caught me in her arms. "Hey this is nice," I said softly. Then she pointed behind me.

"Where are you two supposed to be?" said a voice I knew only too well before I could turn around. Mr. Newley. The principal. I looked back at Glenda, but she hung her head again.

"Listen," I whispered to her, "Go back to class. I'll see you in the parking lot after school." She tried to protest, but I pushed her around the corner and turned to face Newley who was only a foot or so behind us. "How are you, Mr. Newley?" I said, smiling uncomfortably.

"Where is she going?" He gestured after Glenda.

"Back to study hall, sir. We were on our way there, just now. I figured you'd probably want to talk to me rather than to her, sir."

"You figured right. Somebody yelled an obscenity at the librarian a few minutes ago, Charlie. You wouldn't know anything about that, would you?"

"Uh, yes sir, I would." I didn't say anything more.

"You wouldn't want to tell me who that person was, would you, Charlie?" He took a step closer so that his face was only inches from mine.

"Well, sir, not particularly."

I thought he almost smiled. "Well, let's step down to my office," he said, turning and leading the way. As we went into his office, I remembered a time earlier in the year when I had taped a sign over his doorway:

"Abandon hope, all ye who enter here."

It was funny then.

I closed the door at his request. "Sit down, Charlie." He gestured at a chair facing his desk.

I sat. He sat at his desk. We looked at each other. I looked at the floor. When I looked up again, Mr. Newley was looking at me. I knew I had to talk. I leaned forward and rested my elbows on my knees. "Well, sir, it's like this"--

The phone rang. Mr. Newley answered. When he hung up, he excused himself, saying he'd be back in about five minutes. While he was gone, I sat there looking around. I looked at the plaques on the wall, his college diplomas, a picture of his family on his desk--junk like that. But then I spotted something that made me get up and go over to look closer.

On an end table in one corner of his office was a miniature reproduction of Rodin's *The Kiss*. I went over, picked it up, and studied it closely. I knew it from culture lessons in French II, but I was surprised that Mr. Newley had it in his office. I was still standing there holding it when Mr. Newley came back. "Do you like that statue, Charlie?" he asked, watching me closely.

"Yes sir. I like it a lot," I said. I wasn't nervous or anything. I knew what I wanted to talk about.

"You ready to talk?" He'd read my mind.

"Yes sir." I held out the statue. "May I use this?"

"Surely."

I went back to my seat. I pulled it closer to Mr. Newley's desk. I set the statue on the edge of the desk and rested my hands on either side of it. "Well, uh, first I want to say that I was the one who called Mrs. Ralston a--bitch, so I know I've got a big problem here. But I did it for a reason. I mean, I'm sort-of 'guilty with an explanation,' as they say in court."

Mr. Newley looked intrigued, so I went on. "You think of this statue as a work of art, right? Well, I do, too. So does Teddy. Even Ralph does...."

"You mean Teddy Hatter and Ralph Dodge, I take it?" he interrupted.

"Yes sir. Well, I think that makes us a little different from most of the guys. When Miss Slater talked about this statue in French class, most of the guys made crude jokes and stuff, you know? But when Teddy and Ralph and I were talking about it later on, when we were out riding in Ralph's car, we all sort of agreed that it was really beautiful. It was sort of like Keats says in his poem, 'A thing of beauty and a joy forever.'"

"A thing of beauty *is* a joy forever," he corrected. "Interesting, Charlie. But how does this explain why you called Mrs. Ralston a b-that name?"

I smiled even though I tried not to. "Well, sir, it's like this. I was in the library doing some research for a paper in Mrs. Raker's class. Glenda Faire, you know, was in there, too. Anyway, I've had the blues for a couple of day because my girlfriend broke up with me" —

He raised his eyebrows.

"Oh, she doesn't go here to school. I met her at the beach. She's from Charlotte. Her name's Paula." He gave me a look that I knew meant to get to the point. "Well, anyway, Glenda asked me to sit with her, so I did, and she asked me why I was sad, and the next thing I knew she was holding my hand, sort of like a friend, you know? And Mrs. Ralston jumps us and acts like we're going to have sex on the table there any second. So she throws us out of the library, then, to add insult to injury, she yells at us about trying to sneak books out of the library without checking them out. I've never even had an overdue book. She made us both feel like dirt. I mean, I didn't give her any static about her throwing Glenda and me out of the library. So when she did that stuff about the books, I just let her have it."

Mr. Newley leaned back in his chair and tapped his fingertips together. "So," he said, "when someone treats you unfairly, you feel justified in retaliating, even if that retaliation is in itself harmful to you or to others. Is that what you're saying, Charlie?"

I scratched my head. That was probably what I was saying, although that wasn't what I meant at all. I decided to try again. "Well, not exactly. I mean, it wasn't so much that she got after me. I know teachers have to do that stuff. That's what they're paid for."

Mr. Newley smiled again.

"It was the fact that she treated Glenda and me like sex fiends. I mean, when I was talking to Glenda, I took her hand. I just did it as a form of communication, of showing her I cared about what she was telling me. I didn't like Mrs. Ralston dirtying it up the way she did."

Mr. Newley pursed his lips and rubbed his hands together. He wrinkled his forehead as if he were thinking hard. Finally, he said, "Charlie, you're a bright fellow. One of our best thinkers, possibly. But this is the third time this year I've had to call you in about outbursts like this. It's hard to be seventeen. I know that. It's especially hard if you're a sensitive person such as you seem to be. But there are certain social conventions that must be observed. Respect for adults and, especially, respect for authority must be maintained. You understand that, don't you, Charlie?"

"Yes sir," I muttered. Then a thought hit that panicked me. "Uh, Mr. Newley, you're not going to-uh-suspend me are you?" My dad would kill me.

He considered. "No, Charlie," he said after what seemed like ten years. "I don't think that will be necessary. What I have in mind might not even seem like punishment in the usual sense. But it will take a lot of hard work on your part to fulfill your obligations satisfactorily."

"Yes sir." He had me going.

"Here's what I want from you, Charlie. I want on my desk Thursday morning, typed, with footnotes, a five-page report on the artist Rodin and his work. You might especially want to mention *The Kiss*."

Relief spread through me. "Yes sir. No problem. I'll get it in early, if I can." I couldn't believe I was getting off so easily.

"One other thing, Charlie."

I knew it.

"I want a written apology given to Mrs. Ralston-hand delivered-no later than tomorrow morning by eight-thirty. Agreed?"

"Yes sir." Like I was going to argue.

He gestured and I knew it was time to go. I got up and went to the door. As I opened the door to leave, I turned. Mr. Newley had picked up the statue and was studying it, shaking his head thoughtfully. I knew I wanted to say something to show a little gratitude, but I didn't know what. "Mr. Newley?"

"Yes? Something else, Charlie?" He put down the statue, took off his horn-rimmed glasses and rubbed his eyes.

I gestured at the statue. "It's a nice statue, sir."

"Thank you, Charlie."

I felt pretty good about that.

By the time I got back to Miss Harrold's room, 6th period was well underway. I gave her my library note, tried to explain what had happened, and got more good news. She took my library privileges for three weeks. That meant no library work except before and after school, when practically no one except Mrs. Ralston and me would be in the library. I really looked forward to that.

I went to 6th period, French class, and Miss Slater chewed me out about being late. Then she recommended a couple of books on Rodin, and even loaned me one of her own. Finally, I got to my seat and was trying to establish a bit of normalcy. Ralph was in my French class. He sat two seats back, with Tammy Scarsdale in between. He started whispering as soon as I sat down.

He leaned around Tammy. "Hey, where you been, boy?"

"Newley's office."

"Damn, Charlie. What did you do now?"

I shrugged nonchalantly. "I called Mrs. Ralston a bitch." Tammy's eyes widened.

"Bull shit." Ralph slumped back into his seat, disgusted.

I twisted in my seat to face him. "No, it's not. I called Ralston a bitch, and Newley caught me and took me to his office, and we had this discussion, and now I've got to write a term paper on the artist Rodin."

"You're kidding." Ralph shook his head doubtfully.

"No, I'm not. Mr. Newley and I talked about art and stuff, and then he told me I had to write this paper-"

"Jean-Paul! Berton! Allez au front, s'il vous plait." Miss Slater's voice whistled in our ears.

Ralph looked at me. I looked at him. We looked across the room. Miss Slater was looking at us. So was everyone else. We got up slowly and shuffled to the front.

Miss Slater paced before us. "Messieurs. Dites a la classe le sujet de votre discution."

"Well," I began.

"En francais, s'il vous plait!" She scowled at us.

I looked at Ralph again. He looked at me again. Every one else looked at us again. Miss Slater kept scowling. I knew Ralph wouldn't even try, so I began. "Je, uh, nous parlons d'un experience-"

"Non, Monsieur! Le passe compose, s'il vous plait!"

"Oh, god," went Ralph. "Do it, Charlie. I don't know this stuff."

I knew I had to do it. "Nous parlions d'un experience que j'ai eu dans la bibliotheque. J'ai dit Madame Ralston une--garce."

"Monsieur!"

"Mademoiselle Slater, vous m'avez dit-"

"Pas d'importance! Asseyez-vous!"

We went back to our seats. I knew the French word for bitch because Ralph and I spent time after school when we were supposed to be cleaning up the language lab looking up dirty words en francais in the English-French dictionnaire.

Rather than get the class in any more of an uproar, Miss Slater went on with the lesson and let things slide until the end of our period. Just before the bell rang, she called for Ralph and me to stay after class. When everyone was gone we went up to her desk and she gave each of us a week's cleaning duty in the language lab. She also gave me a lecture on talking dirty.

I got away from Slater and Ralph and made my way to the parking lot. Most of the cars were already gone, but I saw Glenda's little blue Volkswagen sitting over next to the chain-link fence that enclosed the football stadium. I didn't see Glenda. When I turned toward my old Chevelle, there she was leaning against it. I waved and trotted over. "Hi," I said as I reached her.

"Hi yourself. Did you get into a lot of trouble?"

"Me. Nah. I know how to talk to Mr. Newley. He let me off pretty light."

She smiled.

I smiled.

I leaned against the car beside her and looked down toward the football stadium. When I looked back she smiled again. I looked back toward the football stadium.

She stood up straight and said, "Walk me back to my car?"

"Sure." I held out my arm and she took it. We strolled leisurely toward her car, trying to make the walk last longer, me so that I could build my nerve, her for whatever reasons she had. "Listen," I said without looking at her when we'd almost reached her car.

"Yes, Charlie?"

I kicked at a piece of gravel. "Well, tomorrow's Tuesday night. There's a basketball game here, you know."

She leaned her head so that she could smile up at me since I was looking at the ground. "I'm a cheerleader, Charlie. I know when all the basketball games are."

"Oh, yeah." I grinned like a fool. Suddenly she put her face, then her body to mine, and I couldn't think. I didn't want to.

When we let each other go, we were both breathless. "I was in love with a girl from Charlotte," was the first thing I said.

By this time we were leaning against her car, me up against her. It was cold, but I don't think either of us felt it. "What was her name?" she asked softly.

We kissed again. When I came up for air, I realized she'd opened her legs so that the insides of her thighs were rubbing lightly against the outsides of mine. "It doesn't matter," I whispered, kissing her forehead.

"What doesn't matter?" She pulled me more tightly against her and kissed my throat.

"Her name. Oh, god, her name," I mumbled.

A loud whistle froze us. "Go get her, Charlie!"

Glenda peeked around me and whispered, "It's Teddy Hatter and Ralph Dodge."

I turned slowly around. Teddy stood with his hands in the back pickets of his pants, grinning like a Cheshire cat. Ralph had his arms crossed, nodding his head as if he comprehended everything clearly.

"Pick me up tomorrow night at six. The jayvee game starts at six-thirty. You know where I live?"

I looked at her, then at the guys, then at her again. "Yes ma'am. I'll be there." I grinned like a fool again.

"Let's give them something to talk about," she said. She took me in her arms again and gave me a kiss and hug that would have brought a dead man to life. Then she slid away and slipped into her car. I stood like a parked car beside her. The VW roared to life. She rolled her window down. "Call me tonight?"

I smiled. "You bet."

She backed away. She stopped the car. "Got my number?"

"No."

"623-4523." She stopped and wrote it on a scrap of paper and handed it to me.

"Okay."

"Call about eight."

"Okay."

"Bye, Charlie."

"Bye."

She roared off, the VW sputtering clouds of vapor. I walked over to Teddy and Ralph, my hands in my pockets.

"Way to go, Charlie, boy." Teddy punched me lightly on the arm.

I grinned. I couldn't think of anything to say.

"She wants your body, Charlie," said Ralph matter-of-factly.

I kept grinning.

"Charlie, she knows about you and Paula." Ralph's look brought me back to reality.

Suddenly, I had an idea. "Did you two put Glenda Faire onto me?"

Ralph shrugged. "Not really. She mentioned to Teddy sixth period that your girlfriend and you had broken up. He put two and two together. Then he filled her in."

"She was asking lots of questions," Teddy added. "I just told her what I knew. I guess that was a lot. We've talked about Paula and Diana Delight enough. I was just running my mouth. Anyway, it doesn't look like I said anything to turn her off."

I smiled, a little ruefully. "No. She's not cold to me."

"No doubt," said Ralph.

We all laughed. "Let's go to the shopping center and get a coke at Mann's Drug Store," Teddy said. "I can't take this cold much longer."

We walked over to my car. Ralph fell into step beside me. "You get a date with her, yet?"

"Tomorrow night. We're going to the basketball game."

He nodded. "That'll be good." A pause. "Charlie?"

"Yeah?"

"I'm sorry about you and Paula. You know?"

I nodded. "I know."

We got to the car and I opened the passenger side door. Ralph crawled into the back seat. Teddy stood outside the car as I unlocked my door. "Charlie?"

"Yeah?" I looked at him and saw what he wanted to say. "Thanks, Teddy. Ralph already said something as we were walking over here."

He smiled. "Have a good time with Glenda." Then a little sadly, "That's all you can do."

"Yeah."

We got into the car and went to the drug store. Ralph bought me a vanilla Coke. Teddy bought me a girlie magazine. I threw the magazine out the car window as I drove home.

I did all the punishment for Mr. Newley.

I got an "A" on the paper on Keats.

Mrs. Ralston never really forgave me.

I didn't care.

Glenda was good to me and I almost forgot Paula.

I got over my blues.

I never really thanked Glenda.

Until now.

TEDDY AND DIANA

"Ain't nothing in the world
Like a big-eyed girl...."

The Big Bopper

I

I used to go fishing pretty often. There was a spot down on the River Road where you could park your car and walk down the east bank of the Dan River to a nice comfortable place behind a big rock. I used to go there a lot. I used to do it not so much because I wanted to catch fish, but because I liked to sit and dream.

Teddy used to come down to the river when I was there fishing. He always brought his guitar, a Fender Stratocaster that he'd sanded down to the bare wood, then varnished. He'd sit on the bank next to me and play, making that tinny sound that electric guitars make when they're not hooked up to amplifiers. Sometimes he'd stop in mid-song to ask me some crazy question or other.

One day in March, Teddy came down to the river. It was hot, and I had some bottles of pop tied on a string and hanging down in the river. I was just opening one when Teddy showed up. I handed it to him.

"Thanks, Charlie." He took a long pull at it. Then he stared off across the river. He had his guitar, and, after staring for several minutes, he shook his head like someone waking up and took it out of its case. He scratched around in his wallet and came out with a pick. He strummed a few tinny chords and fiddled with the tuning pegs. He reached and got his Dr. Pepper, took another slug, gargled with it, and set it down in a safe place. He leaned over his guitar and began playing an old blues tune, "Four until Late." After a bit he sang:

"A woman's just like a dresser/

Someone's always going through her drawers--"

"Boy, that's a good line," I said.

Teddy stopped playing. "Charlie, let me ask you something."

I leaned back on my elbows. "Go ahead."

"Charlie-" he hesitated. "Aw, hell, forget it."

"What?" I can't stand for someone to start to say something and not finish. "Come on, Teddy, what were you going to say?"

"Well, listen." He doodled on his guitar. "Charlie, do you believe—I feel like a fool—do you believe in love?" He stopped again.

"Oh, yeah," I said sarcastically, "I believe in love. I ain't got no doubts about its existence." I reeled in and checked my bait.

He looked across the river. "What I wanted to ask was, do you believe in love at first sight?" I tried to catch his eye, but he wouldn't look at me.

"Well, Teddy"—I couldn't say. It hadn't happened to me. I thought about Paula. I believed in love. "Yeah," I said evenly, "I guess I kinda do."

He looked at me gratefully. "I do too, Charlie. I didn't used to, but I do now. I mean, it's like you meet this girl, you know, and the first time you meet her it's like you've known her a long time. You just go up to her and start talking. And the weird part is, she acts the same way." He talked faster and faster. "Why, we must have talked twenty minutes before I thought to ask her name. And later, when we were parking-"

"Whoa!" I grabbed my rod, dancing with a fish on it. I got control of the situation, put the fish back into the water, and turned to Teddy. "Now, let's go back a minute. Number one, who are we talking about? Number two, when did you meet her? Number three, how did we get to the parking part so quickly?"

"Okay." Teddy played his guitar for a minute. "Her name is Diana Delight. She goes to Reidsville High." He looked off across the river again. "It was Friday night. You were dating Denise-"

"Don't remind me."

"What's the matter? Go badly?"

"You kidding? Houdini couldn't get in. I took her to the movies, then out for pizza, and all I get is a few lousy French kisses and a lot of 'please, no, Charlie'." I tell you what. Sometimes women just make me sick."

Teddy crashed a chord on his guitar. "I got a song about you, Charlie," he said, getting to his feet:

> Look out all you b-uh-witches,
>
> You'd best be up front,
>
> And tell Charlie Beagle,
>
> If you ain't gonna give him — lovin'….

"That's terrible, Teddy." I stood and stretched. Teddy liked it though, so he sang it again. He turned to me. The look on his face was so ridiculous I had to laugh. He got tickled and started snickering. That made me laugh even more. We got to laughing so hard that we had to sit down. Teddy knocked over his bottle of pop and lost almost half of it. Finally we settled down and had some beans and franks with crackers. While we were eating, it occurred to me to get Teddy back on the subject of Diana. "Listen," I said, "you never did finish telling me about Diana. What happened?"

"Well," he munched a cracker, "you were out with Denise having the time of your life--" I winced and he laughed- "so Ralph and I decided to cruise over to Reidsville to look for some action. Anyway, we got to Hardee's and decided to stop because there were a lot of Reidsville High kids there. Ralph was hungry, as usual, so we went into the restaurant to get something to eat. Anyway, we're standing in line and I look over and there she is. Just like that. I looked at her twice, then she looked at me, and then I just went over to her and started talking. She was with her sister, so Ralph got up with her while I was talking to Diana. Ralph and the sister didn't hit it off too well, though. I think she's more your type. That's why I'm here--sort of."

I smelled it coming. "You're not trying to set me up with a blind date, are you, Teddy?" I looked at him disgustedly.

"Come on, Charlie." Teddy rubbed his arm nervously. "You'll like this girl. She's real attractive. Smart, too. Right up your alley. If you want to, we can go talk to Ralph this afternoon. He'll tell you the same thing. I know he will."

I looked away from Teddy. I knew if he were serious enough to let me talk to Ralph about the girl, she must be okay. "Okay, I'll talk to Ralph tonight." I turned back to fishing.

Teddy jumped up. "Let's go now."

"Why?"

"Well, I kind of wanted you to double date with me tonight. In fact, I already set it up with Diana and her sister." He smiled sheepishly.

I was about to laugh at him, but I pretended to be irate. "What? How about if I have a date already?"

He looked stricken. "You don't, do you? Come on, Charlie, this is important to me. Can you get out of the other thing?" It was sort of fun to see Teddy the joker so wrought up, but I couldn't hold out on him. "Well, I don't really have a date tonight." I stroked my chin. "Okay. I'll do it. But I get to talk to Ralph first. Agreed?"

"Sure. Okay. Let's go see him. It's four o'clock now, and we have to pick them up at seven." Teddy was really excited. I'd never seen him act that way over a girl.

"All right. Boy, Teddy, this isn't like you." He had packed his guitar and was heading up the riverbank. I don't think he even heard me. I reeled in my line and put my stuff into my old knapsack. I picked up my tackle box and clambered up the bank. Teddy had already put his guitar in his car and had the motor running. He sat anxiously behind the wheel.

"Listen," he said, "come on over to my house and we'll drive over to Ralph's together." He patted the steering wheel with his hands as he talked.

I followed Teddy over to his house. I parked my car and jumped in with Teddy. Before we could back out of his driveway, his mother came out onto the front porch and called to us. "Teddy! Teddy Hatter!"

He stopped the car, gave me a 'what now?' look and answered. "Yes, Mother?"

"Teddy, are you going to change the spark plugs in my car? You promised you'd do it this afternoon." She rubbed her hands on her apron.

"I'll do it tomorrow." He looked at me and rolled his eyes.

"Tomorrow's Sunday. That's no day for work like that. You've got church."

"I won't do it until tomorrow afternoon. After church. I'll see you later." He backed out into the street.

"Teddy! Teddy! Get a loaf of bread while you're out." He never heard her. We were already out in the street and heading for Ralph's.

"What did she say?" He shifted gears.

"She said to get a loaf of bread."

"Okay. Let's get a beer, too." He stepped on the gas and we raced under a yellow light.

"Now? Why not wait until we're on the way to pick them up?"

"Advance preparation. Besides, we can take one to Ralph." We stopped at G & J Quik Mart. Teddy went in and bought three beers and a loaf of bread. When we got to Ralph's, he'd just finished mowing his lawn. He climbed into the back seat and we headed out of town. We rode out past the fair grounds toward Martinsville, Virginia, each of us sipping a beer.

"I turned to Ralph. "So. Tell me about Diana's sister."

"Dottie? Well, Charlie, she's your type. Nice looking, great body, smart." Ralph never minced words.

"No kidding?" I said. "She's really like that?"

"Charlie," Ralph leaned over the back of the front seat, "I won't lie to you or for you. Unless, of course, it's necessary for your own good."

Teddy flipped his beer can over the top of the car with his left hand. "Well, what do you think?"

"If Ralph says okay, it's okay by me. Stop sign coming up." I drained the last of my beer and handed the can to Ralph. He waited until Teddy gunned the car through the intersection. Then he threw the can at the stop sign. It careened loudly off the sign and into the side-ditch. We exited, tires screaming.

II

I was trying to decide whether to wear English Leather or Canoe when I heard my mother tell Teddy that I was in my room. I splashed on English Leather. Teddy breezed into the room wearing a smile I knew could only have come from Milwaukee. "We're both dead meat if my parents notice you're drinking, boy."

"My, you smell lovely. What is that?" He picked up a cologne bottle from my dresser.

"I'm wearing English leather. That's Canoe. Don't drop it."

"Can I put some on?" He was already unscrewing the top.

"I reckon you can. Hurry up. Let's get out of here." Teddy put some cologne in his hand, but as he tried to set the bottle back on the dresser, he tipped it over. He grabbed it up awkwardly so that it flew out of his hand and threw cologne all over his shirt. I grabbed the bottle and set it on the dresser. "Teddy, you idiot," I hissed. "Look at your shirt."

"Charlie Beagle, that's no way to talk to your friend." My mother's voice rushed in from the hall.

"Sorry, Mom." I scowled at Teddy. "See what you're gonna get us into?"

"What about my shirt, Charlie?" Teddy had that look of tragedy that hits drinking people for trivial reasons.

"I'll lend you one of mine. Let me look in the drawer and find one." Teddy pulled his shirt off. I got out my favorite blue shirt and handed it to him. "If that don't make her come across, nothing will," I said.

"Don't say that kind of stuff, Charlie." Teddy's face became downright stern. I thought of Paula again.

"Let's go." I led the way out, yelling goodbye to my mom. As we got to the car, she called from the back door. "Y'all drive carefully."

"We will."

"Don't stay out too late."

"We won't."

"Have a good time."

"We will."

Teddy gunned the car out of my driveway. I opened a beer and started trying to catch up.

III

By the time we got to Diana's house, we were both primed for action. I'd had two beers and Teddy'd had his third. We walked ceremoniously up onto the porch. Teddy leaned on the doorbell until I pulled him off it. Diana came to the door, called out, "They're here," and pushed us back as she hurried outside. Her sister was right behind her.

"Hi," Diana said.

"Hi," said Teddy.

The sister looked at me. I looked at her.

"Hello," I said.

"Hello, yourself," she said.

"Oh, I forgot," Diana intervened. "Who is this again, Teddy?"

"This is my other best friend, Charlie Beagle."

"Okay. Charles, this is my sister, Dorothy. Dorothy, Charles."

"Dottie."

"Charlie."

I took her arm and we led the way out to the car.

"Why are all these beer cans in the floor of the car?" asked Diana, looking at the car's rear floorboard.

"They had beer in them," Teddy said simply.

"Well, they're empty now." Diana drummed her fingers on the front of Teddy's shirt.

"I know." Teddy smiled.

Dottie looked at me seriously. "Have you been drinking, too?"

"Two. That's all." I held up four fingers.

"Well, I don't know if I want to go out with someone who drinks," said Diana sarcastically.

"It certainly is disgusting," Dottie added.

"Well. I'm so sorry," said Teddy. "Let me leave and spare your sensitive feelings." He opened the car door and got in, slamming it hard. He looked up at me. "You going with me?"

"Where are you going?"

To get a beer."

"Let's go." I went around the car and got in. "Nice meeting you," I said to Dottie, leaning over Teddy and talking out the driver's side window.

"Teddy-"

"What?"

"Why don't we get a couple of six packs and go to the drive-in?"

"That's a great idea."

"Charlie?"

"Yeah."

"Get into the back seat so that these women can get in here with us."

IV

We had a great time that night. We never went to the drive-in, and we never bought the beer, but we had a great time anyway. We wound up driving all the way to Danville, Virginia, thirty miles away, because Teddy and Diana decided that they had to have tutti-frutti ice cream and Teddy knew this place in Danville that sold it. When we got there, they both bought double scoop cones of tutti-frutti, hated them, threw them away, and bought fudge ripple. True love.

We double dated several more times. Dottie and I really liked each other, but when we kissed I knew she wasn't the one, so I let that part of it go. Teddy and Diana just got more and more intense. Ralph and I got to the point after a month or so that we didn't even try to do things with him on the weekends.

I was down at my fishing spot one cool April afternoon when Teddy showed up. I was pretty surprised. I hadn't seen him on a Saturday afternoon for a while. "Well, Romeo, howfore hast thou been?" I said, reeling in my line.

No response. Teddy just kept standing beside me holding his guitar case and looking at the river. Finally he sat down, took out his guitar, and began playing "Love in Vain." When he finished, he sat and strummed chords for at least half an hour. I kept waiting for him to say something, but he never spoke. I stood up, stretched, yawned, and scratched myself. I walked up and down the river bank a while. Finally, I asked him. "When did she break it off, Teddy?"

He didn't say anything. "Then he started to play "Love in Vain" again. He stopped in the middle, put his guitar away, and asked me if he could fish. I was surprised, but I went up to my car and got a rod and reel from the trunk. We fished silently for twenty minutes or so. Teddy caught a fish, but I had to take it off the hook for him. "Charlie," he said as I tossed it back into the river, "I think I'm going to die." Then he cried. Manly, dignified, silent crying. The tears ran down his face while he stared at the river. Once in a while he would rub his face on the sleeve of his shirt. During all this I just sat there. I didn't know how to act while he was crying. I was afraid that if I spoke I'd embarrass him. So I stared at the river, too. The motion of the water made me sleepy, so I lay back on the bank with my hands behind my head. When I woke up, it was getting dark and Teddy was gone.

V

I had just gotten home from another hopeless date with Denise when I heard a car in the driveway. It was Teddy. I watched from the window and saw him get out of his car and start unsteadily toward the house. I went out the back door to head him off. I figured he was drunk and would get us both into trouble. "Hi, Teddy," I said as I met him.

"Come on," He pulled me by the arm.

"Where to?" I tugged away from him.

"Got to go see Diana." He grabbed me again.

"Listen, Teddy, it's eleven-thirty at night. Her folks are going to get really upset if we show up over there, especially with you drinking."

He looked at me for a long moment, then turned and started away. "Going now. You coming?" he said over his shoulder.

I rubbed my hand over my face. "Yeah. Let me get my coat and tell my folks. Wait here." I went in and got my coat. I told my dad I was going with Teddy to his house.

"It's mighty late. When will you be back?" He tapped his cigarette on his ashtray and kept his eyes on the television.

"I don't know. I might spend the night, if it's all right."

"You need to go to church tomorrow." He turned to me and drew on his cigarette.

"I'll go with Teddy. He'll come with me to Youth Group tomorrow night."

He smashed out the cigarette. "All right. Be here for lunch—bring Teddy, if you like," he added after a pause.

I smiled at Dad's gruff kindness. "Thanks, Dad." I stopped by my room and got a pair of dress slacks and a shirt.

"What's all that stuff?" asked Teddy as I threw my things into the back seat.

"I'm going to spend the night at your house. It was the only way I could get out."

"Okay." Teddy gunned the car out of the driveway and spun wheels leaving the house.

"My dad will love that," I said sarcastically.

"Can't help it." Teddy shrugged.

"Damn, Teddy. Talk about it. It will do you good."

Teddy looked at me, his eyes flashing in the beam of oncoming headlights. "I talked like hell this afternoon. Then I looked over at you and you were out like Sleeping Beauty. I ain't talking no more. I'm acting."

"What do you mean?" I turned on the seat to face him. "I know that tone, Teddy. It always gets me in big trouble."

"I'm going over to Diana's house and make her come out with me." He flexed his shoulders.

"You're gonna do what!?"

"I'm gonna go get Diana because I love her."

"Teddy, you're crazy. Old Man Delight is liable to shoot you down like a rabid dog."

"I'm going anyway. Maybe he will. It'd be all the same to me now."

I shook my head. "Lord, Teddy, you've lost your mind. What if she don't love _you_? What if she was the one who wanted to break it off?"

"She didn't. I mean, she did, but it was because her parents made her. I found that much out from my mom. Mrs. Delight called my mother and told her that they'd made Diana break up with me because they felt we weren't good for each other. So I'm going to go get her."

"Heathcliff and Catherine," I murmured to myself.

"What?"

"Never mind. I read too much." I turned and looked out the window. We were halfway to Reidsville.

Teddy reached behind him and felt around on the back seat. "Charlie, reach back there and get the beer," he said.

"Teddy, I don't think you ought to drink any more tonight-"

"Dammit, Charlie, stop being a Boy Scout and hand me a beer."

I reached into the bag. He had a whole six-pack, still pretty cold. As much for my own protection as for any other reason, I began drinking beer as fast as I could. By the time we got to Diana's street on the far side of Reidsville, I had a good buzz on. I knew that because I was starting to look forward to the coming confrontation.

Teddy whipped the car into the Delights' driveway. He cut the lights, jumped out, and slammed the door so hard that the window glass rattled. He'd left the motor running. I sat there perfectly relaxed waiting for the action to begin. Teddy bounded up the front steps and beat on the front door. After a couple of long minutes a light came on and Old Man Delight stuck his head out. Instinctively I drew back a little. Delight had always looked at Teddy and me as if he wanted to kill us. They were talking, but I couldn't quite make out what they were saying. I rolled down the driver's side window.

"I want to see your daughter 'cause I love her." Teddy was really loud.

"I don't give a damn who you love." Mr. Delight was even louder.

"Well, I don't give a damn who *you* love!" yelled Teddy. "I want to see your daughter! Now!"

"I'm going to call the damn police if you don't get the hell out of here right now!" Delight shook his fist in Teddy's face.

"Go ahead! Call the damn law! I'll be gone before they get here!" Teddy shook his fist at Delight.

"You little son of a bitch! I ought to shoot you!" yelled Delight.

"You ain't got the guts!" Teddy sneered.

"We'll see about that, by god!" I heard the door slam. Then Teddy was beating on it again, yelling for Diana to come out. The porch light flashed on, the door swung open, and Delight stood there, mighty and wrathful, shotgun in hands. "Now," he said menacingly. "Are you going to leave, or am I going to blow you away from here?" He leveled the shotgun at Teddy's chest.

I thought Teddy was going to say something else, but then I heard Diana's voice call out from somewhere. "Run, Teddy! He'll do it!"

Teddy didn't waste time. He hurdled the boxwood beside the front steps and hit the ground in full stride. He flung open the car door and came crashing in, knocking me back over on my side of the car. He gunned the motor, slammed into reverse, and screeched back out of the driveway. Suddenly he slammed on brakes. We sat there with the motor running. We could just barely hear the sound of Delight's laughter. Teddy cut the motor, opened his door, and stood on the doorjamb. "I'll get you yet, you old bastard!" he yelled.

"You damn hoodlum! Here's what you get-" I heard the gun go off, and I saw Teddy fall. I could hear shotgun pellets whiz over the top of the car. I froze for a second, scared to look at Teddy for fear Old Man Delight had killed him. Just as I began to move cautiously toward him, Teddy came crashing into the car again. He fired up the engine, slammed into first, and we took off. For a while I felt detached, as if it weren't happening to me. It wasn't until we pulled off Highway 14 and drove down under the Harry Davis Bridge just outside Eden that I began to come to myself.

The car lurched to a stop on the riverbank and we sat there for a few minutes with the motor still running. Teddy eased the gearshift into neutral and pulled up the hand brake. He slumped down in his seat. I had already slumped, so we faced each other, the sides of our faces against the backrest. "You damn near got us both killed," I said quietly.

"Yeah. I know."

"Really. I mean, we're lucky we're not both dead." I shifted a little on the seat.

"I know, Charlie, I know." He looked out the window at the river.

"Tell me something," I said.

"What?"

"Did he shoot at us once or twice?"

He turned to me and grinned. "Hell, I don't know. I went into shock after the first time."

"I smiled and punched him lightly on the arm. "He's a sorry shot, ain't he."

He chuckled softly, "Yeah, He's a sorry shot." He leaned over the seat and fumbled in the back floorboard. He pulled up two tall beers. "Voila."

I took the beer, but I wasn't satisfied. "Well, what about Diana?"

He sighed. "I guess that's over with for sure, now."

I tried to see his face "Does it hurt, yet?"

He popped the top off his beer can. "No. Not yet. The anesthetic hasn't worn off."

The only other sound for a while was me opening my beer, an occasional car on the bridge overhead, and the river.

VI

There was hell to pay for that little outing. When we got back to Teddy's house, it was about two o'clock in the morning. Teddy's dad was waiting up for us. "Where have you two been?" he asked casually, tapping his pipe on the fireplace hearth in their den.

"Just out riding around," Teddy answered calmly.

Mr. Hatter calmly refilled his pipe from the humidor on his desk in the corner. "Really? Where have you been riding?"

"Just around. Out in the country and all." I stood in the doorway, head down. If Teddy didn't know we were caught, I did.

"Diana's father called me. You didn't happen to go by there, did you?" He cut his eyes at Teddy.

"Well, yes sir, we did." Teddy glanced back at me. I shrugged. "We didn't stay long though," he added, putting his foot up on the hearth and staring at the ashes in the fireplace.

Mr. Hatter took his pipe from his mouth and pointed it at Teddy. "No, I didn't think you did. It took a bit of talking to get Mr. Delight to say he wouldn't press charges against you for trespassing. If he hadn't let slip that he took a shot at your car, you'd be in jail by now. I think it would be a good idea if you stayed away from Miss Diana Delight from here on out."

Teddy went to the window and looked out at the darkness. I stood in the doorway kind of dumbfounded.

"Hadn't you better be getting home, Charlie?" Mr. Hatter looked at me in a way that made me turn for the front door.

"Charlie's supposed to spend the night with me," Teddy said flatly.

"Well, I think he'd better go home tonight," Mr. Hatter said evenly.

"He doesn't have his car," Teddy said.

"Then you take him straight home and come straight back," Mr. Hatter said. His tone was more like my father's.

Teddy didn't answer. He walked over to me. "We'd better go," he said.

As we drove back to my house, I wanted to ask Teddy what his father might do. I finally got nerve just as we pulled into my driveway. Before I could ask, he answered.

"Charlie-"

"Yeah?"

"You probably shouldn't call my house tomorrow. Warn Ralph, too, will you?"

"Sure. Okay." I opened the door and got out of the car.

"Charlie-" He put his car in neutral.

"Yeah?" I stood leaning into the harsh light of the car's interior.

Teddy looked at me, his dark brown hair tousled, his blue-gray eyes weary. His long, mobile face was creased and rubbery. "Thanks for going with me and all."

"You're welcome."

"You reckon your folks will be mad?" he said.

"I won't know 'til I go in. I hope they're not awake."

"Good luck." He smiled sadly.

"You, too." I closed the car door quietly. Teddy backed gently out of the driveway and eased away.

I let myself in—silently, I thought—and tiptoed to my room. As I turned the doorknob, I heard my mother's voice. "Charlie, is that you?"

"Yes, ma'am," I whispered hoarsely.

"Come here a minute." I tiptoed to the doorway of their room. The door was open and I could see the lighted tip of my father's cigarette.

"Why are you home, son?" asked Mother.

"Uh, Mr. Hatter thought it would be a good idea if I came home instead of staying."

True.

"Teddy and his folks are going off tomorrow or something."

Possible.

"It's two-thirty in the morning, boy," my dad growled.

"Is it that late? We were asleep for awhile."

A lie.

"Mr. Hatter called here about one-thirty and wanted to know if you all were here," my mother said. She didn't have to say more.

"We went over to Diana Delight's house. She's — she was Teddy's girlfriend. Anyway, Mr. Delight and Teddy had this argument and Mr. Delight cussed Teddy and Teddy cussed Mr. Delight. He shot at us and then we went to Teddy's house. But Mr. Hatter was real mad, so Teddy had to bring me home."

"Why did Teddy and Mr. Delight have an argument?" I could hear my mother shift in the bed.

"Well, because Teddy loves Diana and Old Man Delight-"

"Don't be disrespectful, boy." The cigarette waved.

"MR. Delight hates everybody, especially Teddy and me."

"Somehow I don't think you're telling the whole story," my mother said.

"That's all there is to tell. Honest." I held up three fingers like a Boy Scout.

"Well. You go to bed, son," she said. "We'll talk more in the morning."

Suddenly I felt very tired. "Do I have to go to church tomorrow?" I asked softly.

"Boy, I swear-" my father began.

"Charles-"

He sighed. "You don't have to go to Sunday school, but you'd better be at church."

"Yes sir."

I went to bed. A little after I got into bed I heard my dad get up and go to the bathroom. When he went back to bed, I could hear the vague murmur of his and Mother's voices as I drifted into sleep.

THE FOUR LADIES

"Wipe your hand across your mouth and laugh;
The worlds revolve like ancient women
Gathering fuel in vacant lots."

T. S. Eliot

Ralph Dodge, Teddy Hatter and I used to sit in the Boulevard Café and drink syrupy Cokes waiting for Jenny Swan to walk by on her way home from school. We talked every day about going out the door and walking her home. When she passed, though, all we did was surreptitiously follow her with our eyes and picture ourselves saying vague and clever things that would make her smile. That's all we did.

That is, until the four ladies came along. They gave us something else to talk about.

The first time they came into the restaurant was about a month before Thanksgiving. We were sitting at our usual table by the window waiting for Jenny to pass when the first one came in. She pushed open the plate glass door and walked over to the counter. She didn't say anything, and she didn't look to either the right or left. When Calvin, the counterman, didn't come right over to serve her, she began to tap her foot. When it got loud enough, Calvin came over.

"Yes ma'am, Miss Leila," he said as he worked his way over to her, rubbing the counter with a grubby towel. "What can I do for you?"

"Is our table ready?" she asked.

"Yes ma'am. It's your usual table." He hurried down to the end of the counter, took off his apron, tucked his shirt in, and picked up a menu. "Right this way, please ma'am." He began to lead her toward a particular empty table in a roomful of empties. The sight was pretty ludicrous. We all laughed. No one else was in the place at four o'clock in the afternoon and even during the supper rush the place was never over half full.

Calvin went over to a table in the corner and pulled out a chair. He took the lady's coat and kerchief and put them on the coat rack. Then he came back and seated her. She wouldn't sit down until he went back and pushed in the seat for her. Calvin went back to the counter and got a pencil and an order pad. He shuffled over to her table and drawled, "You ready to order now, ma'am?"

"I suppose so," she said, scanning the menu. "What's the special today?"

"Beef stew, Miss Leila. It's real good today, too." Calvin scratched his head with his pencil.

"Well," she said, sighing a little, "bring me a bowl of that and some cornbread.

"How about a vegetable?" Calvin asked. "The Crowder peas look right good today."

"No, just the stew." She reached for the napkin holder on the table, pulled out a napkin, and unfolded it onto her lap.

Calvin went to the kitchen and came out a few minutes later with a steaming bowl of stew sitting on a plate and a basket full of cornbread wedges. He placed those before her. "How about a glass of iced tea, ma'am?" he offered diffidently.

"Yes, I think that would do well for me," she said.

Calvin went over to the counter and fixed her one. He even took a knife and cut the lemon slice so that he could stick it on the glass and make it look fancy. He carefully carried his creation over to her. "Everything all right?" he asked.

"Just fine," she said, taking up her tea. "This stew's real good, Calvin."

He beamed. "Thank you ma'am. My own recipe."

The little scene had played out, so we shifted our attention back to the street--until the next one came in.

"Hello, Miss Dahlia," said Calvin right away, as if he'd been on the alert.

"Good afternoon, Calvin," she said. "Is Miss Leila here?"

"Yes ma'am. Right this way, please."

He took her to the table and seated her to the right of the first lady. The same ritual ensued; he took her order and came back with stew and more cornbread; he went to the counter and fixed her a glass of tea with the lemon stuck on the rim of the glass. He went by to see if everything was all right and she complimented the stew.

As soon as the second lady was settled, a third showed up. Her name was Miss Geneva. Finally a fourth, Miss Pansy came in.

When they began to leave, they simply repeated the process of their coming. Miss Leila called for her check, scrutinized it, fished in her purse and took out enough to pay the bill (and a nickel tip as Calvin told us later), got her coat, and went over to the counter. Calvin rang up the sale and thanked her for the tip. They exchanged pleasantries for a few moments and then Miss Leila announced her departure.

"We'll see y'all later, we're just talking now." She marched out. As she opened the door, she looked over toward us and nodded. We nodded in return. Miss Dahlia, Miss Geneva, and Miss Pansy followed in the same order in which they'd entered. When the last one was gone we practically knocked over tables and chairs getting to the counter to talk to Calvin.

"They always act like that?" Ralph ran his fingers through his long red hair.

"As long as I've known them," said Calvin. "They've been coming here to eat supper six months out of the year for the last five years."

"Where do they go the other six months?" I asked.

"Oh, they eat at the Tarheel Quick Lunch, then." Calvin nodded his head knowingly.

"Got a fixation on fancy restaurants, huh?" said Teddy, grinning slyly.

"Do they always act like that?" said Ralph, plopping onto a stool at the counter.

"Like what?" Calvin cocked his head to one side as he looked at Ralph.

"Coming in one at a time and all, you know, like they did today," I said.

Calvin nodded sagely again. "Yeah. They always do that."

"Why did they start coming here now, in October?" I asked. "Seems like if they were going to go to each place six months of the year, they'd start in January."

"Well," said Calvin, twisting his grimy towel, "it's kind of funny about that. As I remember, they used to go to the Tarheel Quick Lunch all the time. Then about five years ago, it was Miss Pansy's birthday, October 20, so for a birthday present she asked to go to a new restaurant. Well, they came here, and I waited on them pretty much the same as I did today, and they seemed to take it so well that they came back every day for a week. Then they didn't come in for a couple of days and I thought 'Well, that's over with,' but no, the next day they came in, and when I got them served and everything, Miss Leila, she's kind of their leader, she called me over to their table and commenced telling me how they'd decided to eat at this place six months a year, then go to the Tarheel the other six months. Made old Mort over at the Tarheel right sick, I bet." He chuckled to himself. "They been coming here, like I said, about five years now."

"That's really interesting," Ralph said.

"Oh, it's fascinating." Teddy grinned. Ralph punched him lightly on the arm.

"Can't you be serious about anything?" he asked, about to laugh himself.

"It is interesting," I said, nodding my head.

"Oh, come on, Charlie," said Teddy, "don't start that starry-eyed crap with me."

We left the café full of talk about the four ladies. We ruminated on their private lives, laughed at crudities about their bathroom habits, and generally amused ourselves with thinking about four harmless old ladies with eccentric dining tastes. And everyday we went down to the Boulevard Café to watch them. Then one day they didn't come in. We waited around until six o-clock, though we knew they usually came in at four-thirty.

"Maybe they decided to sample the cuisine at Le Quick Lunch de Tarheel," laughed Teddy as we left the café in the gathering darkness.

The next day when we got to the café, Miss Dahlia was standing at the cash register paying Calvin. It seemed strange that she was the only one there, but we went over to our table by the window and sat down. After she'd paid, Calvin handed her a stack of those Styrofoam containers that restaurants put take-out orders in. She started out balancing the stack rather unsteadily in her arms. As she neared the door, Ralph jumped up and went over to open it for her. She smiled and thanked him. As she started through the door, she tripped on the doorjamb and stumbled, losing control of the stack of containers. Ralph went down on one knee and caught the stack just as it slipped from her hands. His kneeling there and her sort of holding her hands down to him reminded me of a picture of Gareth and Lynette I'd seen in an illustrated copy of *Idylls of the King*, a book we'd studied in English literature.

"Why, thank you, young man," said Miss Dahlia, casting her eyes down.

"Uh--you're welcome, ma'am." Ralph looked a bit flustered, but also like he felt like Sir Gareth. He looked up and said, "How about if I carry these home for you?"

Miss Dahlia looked surprised, but nodded assent. Ralph took the containers and stood up to let her pass by first. He followed with the containers. About the time he got to where "Boulevard Café" was painted on the window, Teddy jumped up and went out after him. There we went down the street: Miss Dahlia out front, Ralph behind her with the food, then Teddy, then me. I'd followed Teddy at about the same distance.

We trudged on for four or five blocks. I caught up with Teddy and asked him why he followed Ralph. He said he wanted to find out where Ralph was going. Then he got philosophical. "You know, Charlie," he said, "old people are a lot like teenagers. Folks say we're 'too young to care.' Old people are sort of 'too old to care.' I figure they're just trying to be happy, like we are."

I was pretty impressed by Teddy's speech. I was so impressed, in fact, I almost ran into Ralph who had stopped in front of a small white frame house. It had a front porch with banisters; it was a lot like my grandmother's house. It needed a paint job, though, and when we walked up onto the porch, the flooring had a spongy feeling to it, like it needed rebuilding. Miss Dahlia asked me to knock, so I did. Miss Geneva came to the door.

"Well, this is a surprise." She smiled nervously as she looked at us all.

"Geneva, these nice boys carried our suppers home," said Miss Dahlia. "I thought we might have them in for some cake and milk."

"Well--" Miss Geneva looked at Miss Dahlia. "I guess Leila won't mind."

Miss Dahlia said sharply, "I baked that cake and I bought that milk. Leila has nothing to say about it. Y'all come on in." She took the trays from Ralph and pushed past Miss Geneva into the house. Miss Geneva followed her, pushing the door slightly closed as she went. We stood uncertainly on the porch for awhile, the first cold wind of the fall whipping around the corner of the house. Finally Ralph said, "Aw, to hell with this, I'm going in." He pushed open the door and walked in. Teddy and I weren't far behind. There was an entrance hall and two doors, one on the right a few steps from us, the other further down the hall to the left. Ralph looked in the doorway to the right and said, "Will you look at that?" Teddy and I leaned around him and looked in. Miss Geneva and Miss Dahlia were scurrying around trying to get some elaborate place set up for us to eat a piece of cake. They had put up a card table there in the parlor and were putting a white linen tablecloth on it. Then they put out silverware and real cloth napkins. "Good lord," Ralph said quietly. "I hope I don't make a mess."

Evidently Miss Geneva heard him. She looked up startled, then said, Y'all come in. I bet you thought we'd forgotten you."

"Well, the wind was cold and all..." mumbled Teddy.

We shuffled into the parlor and sat down in cane bottomed chairs. Three teenaged boys at a rickety card table is a chancy business, but we managed to sit through getting served without a disaster. The ladies brought in thick slices of cake and big glasses of milk. It was yellow cake with chocolate icing, homemade, and it was really good. We ate like pigs, two slices of cake each and close to a gallon of milk between us. The ladies had disappeared, reappearing only to provide more cake and milk. Finally Miss Pansy, the youngest looking one, came and stood in the doorway and watched us. Ralph looked up from his cake.

"Do you all live here together?" he asked. She looked surprised at first, but then she decided it would be all right to answer, I guess.

"Yes, we all stay together. Miss Leila thought it would be the best thing. We all get Social Security, which wouldn't support us by ourselves. But together we get by. This is Leila's and my house. We're sisters. Dahlia and Geneva are sisters, too. We're all cousins. So it's just kinfolk."

"Ain't it kind of crowded? This is a right small house." Teddy looked about the room, then at her.

"Well, we do share rooms. I stay with Geneva and Dahlia stays with Leila. But it's our house. All four rooms and the bathroom are ours, free and clear. We only pay for heat, lights, and water--" she cast her eyes down suddenly. "You don't want to hear an old woman rattle on." She looked up and gestured at the table. "Would any of you like more cake or milk?"

We all shook our heads. "No thank you," I said. "But I have a question. Why haven't you all been to the café lately?"

She sighed. "Well, Leila had another of her spells. She's been having them more and more, but she won't go to the doctor no matter how much we fuss and beg."

"Oh." I gave Teddy and Ralph a meaningful look and we all rose. "We didn't mean to bother you with sick folk in the house."

"Oh, honey, that's all right." She waved us back into our seats. "Leila's feeling much better. She was downright cheerful when Dahlia told her y'all had helped carry our suppers home."

"Do you think she'd mind if I said hello?" asked Teddy. Ralph and I looked at him surprised. Teddy wasn't known for his kind heart.

"Why, yes, I think she'd like that," said Miss Pansy. "I'll just speak to her."

She went to the bedroom and came back a few minutes later with a pleased look on her face. "Y'all go right in, " she said.

We got up rather too carefully from the table and stretched, then, with Teddy in the lead, walked down the hall to the bedroom. Teddy stuck his head around the doorway and said, "Hi." We were invited in.

Miss Leila was sitting up in bed. She looked okay to me. Teddy went over and took the chair by her bed and started talking with her to beat the band. Ralph went and leaned against the bedpost and talked with Miss Geneva and Miss Dahlia. I was still standing at the door feeling sort of left out when Miss Pansy touched me on the sleeve. She motioned for me to follow her into the hall. "Would you do something for me?" she asked.

"If I can, ma'am."

"I like to take a walk every evening. Leila doesn't like for me to go out by myself, so I was wondering if you'd go with me." I didn't know what else to do so I said I would. We went by the parlor so I could get my coat. I helped her get hers on and we went out.

We walked for a good thirty minutes and Miss Pansy told me why she never married. It seems she had this fiancé, and he went into the army in 1916. When World War I started for the U.S. in 1917, she was afraid he'd have to go to France and fight. Then she got a letter from him telling her he'd miss all the action because he had to go to Alaska on a surveying expedition. She was really happy when she got that letter, she said, because she thought he'd be safe. Six months later an avalanche on Mount McKinley killed him. She got so teary-eyed telling me that part that I did some cartwheels and other silly stuff to get her smiling again. I shepherded her back to the house. Ralph and Teddy were waiting on the porch. Miss Geneva was standing at the door. As she went into the house, Miss Pansy invited us to return again soon.

We did. We decided sort of unofficially to be the protectors of the ladies. Just like the knights in *Idylls of the King*.

One Friday night we went out to a construction sight and swiped some scrap lumber. We used it the next day to fix their front porch. We went in together and bought a gallon of white paint. It was enough to do the banisters and all of the front of the house. We were sort of sorry after because it made the rest of the house look sad. The ladies liked it, though. They were real nice and appreciative about everything we did.

At Thanksgiving--actually the night after because we spent the real day with family--we had a dinner at the Boulevard Café. Calvin had invited us because he said he appreciated everything we had done for the ladies.

Anyway, we had a nice dinner. Turkey and dressing and all kinds of other stuff Calvin had fixed. We all sat around the big round table at the back of the café. At the end, after the pumpkin pie, Calvin brought out a bottle of homemade wine and we each had a glass. We toasted the ladies, then Calvin. They in turn toasted us.

The week after Thanksgiving Miss Leila got sick again. We took their supper trays over to them and visited a little. By and by she got better, so on a Friday night about ten days before Christmas the ladies came back to the café. Calvin was so happy to see them he set a special table and put a candle on it. He lit it and turned off most of the lights while the ladies ate. We sat and watched for awhile, really enjoying it, but when we were leaving, something happened. I threw open the door and the draft blew out the candle. Everybody was there in the dark for a moment and then one of the ladies, Miss Dahlia, maybe, said, "It's an omen."

On Monday when we went to the café, Calvin was wiping the counter with his grubby towel. He looked up and nodded as we came in and the look on his face told us something was wrong. "Miss Leila's in the hospital," he answered when Teddy asked. "They had to take her in an ambulance last night. She's pretty bad off. They ain't expecting her to live."

We looked at each other in silence. "Can she have visitors?" asked Ralph finally.

"They might let you in. I went this morning." Calvin turned his head and began making furious swipes at the counter with his towel.

We walked over to our table and sat for about twenty minutes. Teddy said we should go see her. We made plans to go that evening.

The drive to the hospital was especially silent, my two questions getting monosyllabic replies. The receptionist told us to go to the second floor. We took the elevator. The nurse at the second floor desk gave us passes that allowed us to visit for fifteen minutes. We walked down the hall looking for Room 211. Then we saw the other ladies sitting on folding chairs outside the door of a room. They nodded their heads in greeting as we came up.

"I told Leila y'all would come," said Miss Pansy.

"It was nice of you boys to come," said Miss Dahlia.

We mumbled "Thank you" and opened the door to the room quietly. Miss Leila was lying in bed in the half-dark room with her head toward the wall. When the light from the hallway reached her face, she turned toward the door. She saw us and smiled. She looked pale and weak. We stood there shuffling our feet, not sure what to say.

"I thank you boys for coming," Miss Leila said softly. "If you don't want to say anything, that's all right. Y'all having come is enough."

We stood looking at our feet and feeling relieved of the burden of small talk. A nurse came and told us our visiting time was over. We mumbled best wishes for Miss Leila's recovery. We turned to go. Then Teddy, in a moment of effusiveness, went over to the bed and kissed Miss Leila's cheek. Ralph and I looked at each other, then at them. Teddy stood there confused, Miss Leila holding his hand. Then she dropped it. "Y'all better go," she whispered.

We re-said good-byes and left. Later, at Empry's Dairy Bar, when we asked Teddy why he'd done it, he shrugged his shoulders.

Miss Leila died the next morning. Calvin told us when we came into the café after school. He told us that the funeral would be the next day.

"Isn't that kind of quick?" asked Ralph.

"Well," said Calvin, "the ladies don't have much money, so it'll be pretty simple. Be easier on them, too. Franklin Funeral Home recommended it."

I recommended that we go to somebody's house and rest up, then go the funeral home that night. Ralph agreed. Teddy didn't say anything. We went over to Ralph's and sat around until about six o'clock. We listened to some music, but none of us talked much. Teddy sat there the whole time holding a Rolling Stones' album cover. Finally Ralph took us home so we could shower and put on coats and ties to go to the funeral home.

About the time I got my tie halfway right, Ralph called. He said he'd called Teddy's house and that Mr. Hatter had said that Teddy had gone out about twenty minutes before. "He could be here at my house in five minutes," Ralph said. "I knew we shouldn't have let him drive. You reckon he's gone off somewhere to get drunk?"

"I don't know." It was possible. "You know Teddy."

"Yeah."

Just then I heard someone at the front door. I heard my mother telling Teddy hello, so I told Ralph that the prodigal had returned. A few minutes later, as we drove to Ralph's, I wanted to ask Teddy why he drove across town to pick me up first rather than going by for Ralph who lived much closer. I didn't though. Some things just seem self-explanatory.

We picked up Ralph and went to the funeral home. The other ladies were there, and Calvin and a couple of guys who looked like ministers. There were three or four other guys there, but I could tell that they were morticians. The ministers came over and invited us to youth fellowship at their churches. Miss Geneva kept admonishing us to go over and "say goodbye" to Miss Leila. We couldn't do it. We just went over to the row of folding chairs that they always have in viewing rooms and sat down, occasionally making sidelong glances at what was left of her.

A few people drifted in and out, but mostly they talked to the ladies, so all we did was sit there and get more uncomfortable. About eight-thirty Neil Franklin came over and asked us to come back to his office. I figured he was going to ask us if we were kin or something and ask us to help out with the bill. Instead, he merely pointed out that there weren't any pallbearers and asked if we'd mind helping out. With Calvin, he said, we'd make four. We shuffled our feet, hemmed and hawed, and agreed. When we came out of the office, Teddy said he didn't want to go back to the viewing room.

"What do you want to do?" I asked.

"Go somewhere," he said.

We slipped out a side door without any good-byes and went around to Teddy's car. He left the parking lot with tires squealing and we tore down Boone Road at about sixty miles an hour. We slid into Kendall's store's parking lot and Ralph went in and bought two six packs. We drove down to the River Road, to the place where I like to fish. When we got there, Teddy grabbed the beer and took off down to the riverbank. It was December, and the wind off the river was cold.

"What are you doing, Teddy? It's cold as hell down here," said Ralph, slapping his arms across his body to warm himself.

Teddy tossed him a can. "Drink a beer. You'll warm up."

"Come on, Teddy, let's go back and sit in the car," I said.

"I'm staying here. If y'all want to go back to the car, go."

We figured if Teddy was going to stay down there and freeze to death, we'd stay with him. We gathered brush and built a fire. We dragged up a log to sit on and commenced drinking. Teddy was right. It got better. After a couple of beers, it didn't seem cold at all. We talked about the ladies, about Jenny Swan, and about lots of other things. Eventually we ended up on the ladies again.

"I guess Miss Dahlia will take over as the head lady now," said Ralph.

"No," said Teddy.

"Why not?" I sat up and looked at Teddy, his face half-lit, half-shadowed.

"It's like the seasons," he said, looking at the river. "You wouldn't expect the world to go on with three seasons, would you?"

Out of the mouths of drunken babes.

VELMA

"More geese than swans now live,
More fools than wise."

Orlando Gibbons

Ralph used to drag me into Piggy's Pool Hall with him all the time. I'm a lousy pool player, and whoever lost had to pay for the game, but that really didn't matter because it only cost ten cents a game, and it was a rare evening if Ralph wanted to beat me more than three or four games in an evening. Usually someone else who could shoot decent pool would come in and I'd be off the hook. Then I'd wander over to the bar in the next room and try to get Alan, the bartender, to sell me a beer to go with the hot dogs I always bought. I invariably drank Pepsi.

Velma used to come into Piggy's all the time. Not many women came into Piggy's, and certainly no ladies did, so that sort of bespoke Velma's reputation right there. The first couple of times we saw each other there we didn't speak, but after a while she began coming over to the booth where I sat with my hot dogs and soft drink. We'd chat a bit, then she'd go over to the bar and have a few beers. Usually some redneck would buy her a beer or two and start whispering to her, and then they'd go out arm in arm, laughing softly between them. Sometimes she came back the same night, sometimes she didn't. The rednecks never did. I looked at her as sort of local color like the Firechief or Dudley, retarded guys who sold White Cloverine Salve for a living.

The night of December 23rd I was sitting home feeling pretty sorry for myself. My father and I had had a fight because I wanted to major in drama in college and my father wanted me to major in business administration. "Can't make no money acting, boy," he said.

I told him I couldn't see going to college to study business. He told me he couldn't pay for somebody to go to college to study acting. We left it at that for a while.

I was sitting in my room listening to Robert Plant of Led Zeppelin yell "Your Time is Gonna Come," wishing it already had. I decided to call around to see if anybody else was home. After the fight I'd refused to go shopping with my dad, mom and little sister, so I was stuck at home. My old Chevelle was in the shop. Teddy and Ralph were both gone out. It was Christmas.

Finally I remembered where my dad kept an extra set of keys for his pick-up truck. I got them and drove downtown, sort of aimlessly riding around. Then I rode by Piggy's. The place was open. I parked Dad's truck up the street by the Grand Theatre so no one would see it outside the poolroom and walked back down to Piggy's.

As I walked down the Boulevard toward the pool hall, I looked at the Christmas decorations attached to the streetlights. They looked really shabby and sad. "God, what a town," I thought. I was still mad about the argument with my dad.

When I pushed open the door to Piggy's bar, I was surprised to find Velma and myself the only customers. Alan explained that the textile mills had paid off and shut down early, and that most of the men were out buying Christmas for their kids. I sat and nursed a Pepsi, trying to imagine one of the hard-handed men I'd seen in the pool hall putting a tricycle or doll carriage together. The thought made me smile absently. Velma noticed, evidently.

"A penny for your thoughts," she said, moving to the stool beside mine at the bar.

"I was just thinking something funny. Kind of a private joke," I answered.

"Oh."

We didn't speak again for a few minutes. Just when I was ready to push away my drink and head home, Velma said, "You used to ride Bus 37. And get off at the Eden Boys' Club. And you used to always talk to Jenny Swan in the school yard at the junior high."

I looked at her, amazed. The fact that Velma could know Jenny Swan struck me as a surprising and faintly odious revelation. "That's right," I said. Then more aggressively, "How did you know all that?" I guess I was trying to intimidate her. Velma wasn't the sort who ruffled easily, though.

"I rode that bus sometimes. You kids must've been in the seventh or eighth grade when I was a senior. You remember me?"

Suddenly I did. I remembered her clearly for the first time. She was a senior girl who used to ride the bus sometimes and about whom all the older boys snickered. I hadn't connected the two: the overdressed, over made-up high school girl and the "professional woman" at Piggy's.

We'd broken the ice, so we started talking about school, about the football and basketball teams, about dances and dates and all sorts of teenaged stuff. We'd been talking maybe fifteen minutes when Alan drew a beer and slid it across the bar to me. "Merry Christmas, kid." He grinned.

"Thanks." I raised the glass in salute, then took a long drink.

Velma laid a twenty-dollar bill on the bar. "Keep them coming, Alan," she said.

He considered a moment, then smiled again. "Okay. But if anyone comes in, the kid's back on Pepsi."

We all laughed. Velma and I resumed our conversation. As the night wore on and the beers took hold, Velma got pretty maudlin and nearly cried when she talked about a boy who had asked her to the senior prom only to back out when the other guys kidded him so much. I got mellow, too, and talked about how much I liked Jenny Swan and how I was too big a coward to tell her. "You should tell her," Velma said.

"I'd feel like a fool," I said.

"You'll feel like a bigger fool if you don't," she said, rapping her mug on the bar for emphasis.

Closing time sneaked up on us. I knew I'd be in trouble for taking the truck out without permission, but I didn't care. Alan ran us out. He tried to give Velma her change, but she wouldn't take it. She kept insisting it was his Christmas present. She kissed him on the cheek and we left the bar. Velma was a little unsteady, and she leaned against me as we walked down the Boulevard.

"Ain't these lights beautiful?" She pointed at the Christmas lights hanging from the streetlights. "If it wasn't for these lights, and the Easter displays at Globman's, and jack o'lanterns on people's porches at Halloween, and things like that, I'd have probably killed myself by now. You know what I mean, Charlie?"

I didn't, so I said nothing. Velma looked at me confidentially. "You ever had a woman, Charlie?"

I didn't know how to answer. I thought I knew what she might suggest next, and I didn't want that, though I did. I finally just grinned sheepishly.

"Yes…no…well, sort of…" I finally got out.

She laughed off-handedly and kissed me on the cheek. "You're all right, Charlie. Jenny Swan's a fool if she won't have you. You're sweet. Really sweet."

She strolled away down the street, making clouds of beery vapor in the night air. "Don't you want a ride home?" I called after her.

She turned and considered me a moment. Then she smiled again. "I'd rather walk, I think." She pointed upward. "So I can enjoy the lights." She waved cheerily and went her way.

I took a step after her, but thought better of it. As I walked up the street toward the truck, I looked at the Christmas lights. They didn't seem half as bad.

One thing bothered me after I got home and into bed. She never did say how she knew Jenny Swan.

DRAGON SLAYING

"Whatever is, is right."

Alexander Pope

"I don't think what you boys are talking about doing is one bit right, and if Raoul comes in here, I'm going to warn him against you." Mr. Austin closed the drink box's lid.

"I'm trying to pick out a drink, man," said Ralph, reopening the lid.

"Well, hurry up. You're letting all the cold air out. It costs money to run that machine."

Ralph dug into the box and pulled out a Double Cola. He closed the lid and put the cap of the bottle against the wooden shelf above the drink box, then knocked the bottle cap off by hitting down on it. When he knocked the cap off, he also tore a chip from the shelf.

"Here, that ain't no way to open that bottle. You boys ain't got a lick of sense." Mr. Austin waved his hands at Ralph as if shooing a chicken.

Ralph shrugged his shoulders and walked over to the rack of marshmallow pies and oatmeal cookies. He picked up an oatmeal cake and bit the cellophane open with his teeth. Just as he flipped it onto the floor while trying to get it out of the package with one hand, Teddy stuck his head inside the store.

"Ralph! Come on! I just saw Raoul Lamb cruise up Bridge Street." Teddy's head disappeared.

"Let's go, Charlie." Ralph put his half-empty bottle into the half-full crate beside the drink box and went out the door.

I tossed 50 cents at Mr. Austin and tore out after Ralph, leaving my own drink sitting on the window seat.

"Here! You boys come on back here! You all are going to get into a mess! Come on back here!" I could see Mr. Austin standing in the doorway of his little store waving at us as I looked through the back window of Ralph's Plymouth while we were driving away.

"Where exactly did you see him, Teddy?" Ralph gunned the car down Spring Street toward Bridge. We turned right on Bridge and rode up past Empry's Dairy Bar. Ralph circled back and cruised through, looking for Lamb's Chevy Bel Air. We were almost through the parking lot when someone called Ralph's name. "Who was that?" He searched the rear view mirror.

"Hold it!" Teddy leaped from the car as it screeched to a halt. He ran around to the front of the Plymouth and got up onto the hood. "Who hollered?" he yelled. A half dozen cars blew their horns.

"Teddy Hatter!" Gary Coverdale got out of his car and climbed onto its hood. "Where y'all going?"

"Queer hunting," yelled Teddy. Laughter and horn blowing.

"You that horny?" yelled Coverdale. Even more laughter and horn blowing. Coverdale waved his clasped hands over his head in victory.

"Naw," yelled Teddy, "just trying to get you a date."

Total uproar. Gary jumped down from his car and ran toward Teddy. Teddy jumped down and went toward him. They grabbed each other in a mock wrestling match. They fell to the pavement and rolled around. Then, suddenly, they stood, brushed themselves off, and spoke briefly. They walked back to their respective cars as if nothing had happened. "Gary said that Lamb hasn't been here tonight," said Teddy as he got into the car. "He said that he saw him in the A & P parking lot when he drove by on the way here, but that was forty-five minutes ago."

"Let's find him."

As Ralph shifted to first and started to move, there came a tap on his window. He stepped on the brake and rolled his window down. Mrs. Empry stuck her head in, her gray hair brushing the roof of the car above the window. "Teddy Hatter, Ralph Dodge, if you two can't do anything but cause problems here, I'd just as soon you stayed away." She glanced at the back seat. "Charlie Beagle, is that you?"

"Yes, ma'am." I slumped in my seat.

"Well, your grandma will hear about this the next time I see her. I'd think you could find something better to do than run around with these two." She pulled her head out of the car.

"All I was doing was sitting in my car," Ralph said in a voice that would drive a nail, it was so hard.

"Don't talk back to me, Ralph Dodge. I'll call your daddy. You've had traffic blocked for the last ten minutes. Y'all fool boys aren't the only customers I have, you know."

"Let me remove myself then." Ralph gunned the Plymouth, popped the clutch, and we squealed out into Bridge Street. I looked back at Mrs. Empry standing dumbfounded in the parking lot.

"Where we going?" Teddy said, looking over at Ralph a little uneasily.

"First to Quik Pik for beer. Then to find Lamb." Even as Ralph spoke he wheeled the car into the parking lot of the convenience store. "Back in a minute." He went into the store.

The entire front of the store was glass, so we could see everything that went on. Ralph took a six-pack from the beer cooler, went to the counter, set it down, and handed the attendant a bill. I could tell from the action that the attendant didn't believe that Ralph was eighteen. Finally Ralph opened his wallet and handed the attendant something. The attendant looked at it, handed it back to Ralph and rang up the sale. When he got out to the car, he tossed the beer to Teddy. I leaned over the back of the front seat. "What happened in there?" I asked as Teddy handed me a beer.

"He carded me." Ralph backed the car around and headed out of town.

"How did you pull it off? I saw you hand him something. I get run out of almost every store I go into."

Teddy opened his beer. "That's because you look about fourteen years old," he said.

"Big deal. You look twenty-five, I'm sure." I slumped back into my seat and opened my own beer.

"What _did_ you show him, Ralph?" asked Teddy.

Ralph didn't answer until we passed the city limits sign and were headed up the Ridgeway Road toward Virginia. "My draft card," he said finally, after a long pull at his beer.

"Bullshit." I took a drink of my own beer.

"Well, Charlie, it wasn't _my_ draft card, of course. I bought it from Gray Vogler a couple of days ago." He shrugged casually.

"A draft card?" Teddy leaned toward Ralph.

"You _bought_ a draft card?" Teddy and I looked at each other astonished.

"From Vogler?" Teddy said, looking at Ralph again.

"From Vogler." Ralph nodded calmly.

"How?" We said in unison.

Ralph shrugged. "I met him in the parking lot at school Thursday afternoon. He wanted some money to get drunk—he's an alcoholic, you know-so he tried to sell me his class ring. I didn't want that, so he asked me if he had anything I would like to buy. I thought a few minutes and realized that a draft card would be invaluable in situations like the one a few minutes ago"— he looked at us and we nodded assent- "so I offered, and he sold it to me for five dollars. By the way, you each owe me fifty cents for beer."

I leaned back in my seat. "Your logical mind never ceases to amaze me, Ralph. I'd never have thought of that. I must have a ten year old brain to go with my fourteen year old body." I looked at my slight frame and shook my head.

"That's it!" Ralph whipped the car into the parking lot of the Ridgeway Steak House. Beer went everywhere.

"What in the -" yelled Teddy.

The car slid to a stop. Ralph turned in his seat. "Get out, Charlie," he said opening his door and leaping out of the car.

"Get out? Why?" I asked through the closed window.

"Just get out. I'll explain." Teddy opened his door and I got out of the back seat. I stood on the passenger's side of the car and stared disgustedly at Ralph standing on the driver's side.

"You got beer on my new alpaca sweater," I said.

"Come around here." Ralph waved me toward him.

"Why?"

"Charlie, you're wasting time."

"Good lord, Ralph." I trudged around to his side of the car.

"Teddy, get around here," Ralph called. Teddy got out of the car, came around on the driver's side, and stood beside Ralph. I stood facing them, three or four feet away.

Ralph turned to Teddy. "If we took his alpaca sweater and gave him a sweatshirt or something, he could pass for twelve years old, couldn't he?"

Teddy shook his head hesitantly. "I'm not sure, Ralph. Charlie's a lot taller than any twelve-year-old is. He pretty much looks seventeen."

"Not if it's almost dark, the way it is right now." Ralph gestured at the dusk.

"Ralph, exactly what do you have in mind?" I was afraid I knew.

"Well, Charlie, here's what I have in mind. We'll dress you up to look like a twelve-year-old kid. We'll put you on the corner of, say, Early Avenue and Bridge Street, over by the DeMolay Building. Teddy and I will park behind the building and keep watch. If old Raoul tries to pick you up, as he always does with young boys alone, we'll get him. You know he always tries to pick up young boys. That's why I'm out to get him. We'll follow him wherever he takes you — usually up in the country somewhere so I hear — we'll move in, and the three of us will teach Raoul a little lesson about bothering little boys."

Ralph hated Raoul Lamb. Raoul had tried to pick up Ralph's 13-year-old cousin Bucky "Spunk" Dodge one afternoon as Bucky walked home from school. Nothing happened (Bucky's nickname suits him admirably; he kicked Raoul's car and ran away), but when Bucky told Ralph about the incident, Ralph resolved then and there to get Raoul Lamb but good. Ralph's that kind of fellow.

"I'm not too crazy about this idea," I said, brushing the sleeve of my sweater. "Besides, we can't do all of that tonight."

Ralph looked at me indulgently. "I know that, Charlie. Tonight we finish our beer and plot strategy. Then, tomorrow evening, about sundown, we put you out as bait and go fishing for a fag."

"Alliteration," I murmured automatically.

"What?" Teddy glanced at me.

I shrugged at them both. "Never mind. I read too much."

Ralph opened his car door to get in. "C'mon. We'll ride out to Big Paul's cabin. Then we'll go back to town and see if we can meet up with some women. Gary Coverdale told me there are some new ones from Mayodan cruising around Eden."

"Ralph?"

He rolled down his window. "Yes, Charlie?"

"I'm still not sure this plan is something I want to be part of."

Ralph gunned the Plymouth's motor. "C'mon, Charlie. Let's go to Big Paul's."

Teddy jogged around to the passenger's side and opened the door. "C'mon, Charlie."

I looked at them both. There was an air of expectation about Ralph, one of anticipation about Teddy. I shook my head. "What the hell." I went around the car and crawled into the back seat.

II

"Listen, Ralph," I said as we drove along.

"What?"

"Why don't we just wait on Lamb on some side street and waylay him? Then we can *all three* get him. Sounds like a good plan to me." I pulled myself up so that I was leaning over the front seat between Teddy and Ralph. I looked from one to the other.

"That might work, at that." Teddy shifted to sit sideways on the seat.

"Won't do." Ralph wheeled the car across a lane of traffic onto the Goat Farm Road.

"Why not?" I whined.

"Well, Charlie, there are two good reasons for doing this my way. First, if we just waylay him, we could get involved in a legal hassle"--he glanced and we nodded"--second, we could spend days, even weeks trying to set up an ambush, only to have it fall through. Just too difficult. Lamb's real suspicious. He's been beaten up before. And if you want a third"--

"Never mind," I said, slumping into the back seat.

We turned off the Goat Farm Road down a winding dirt track that led to a converted tobacco barn known locally as The Cabin. Big Paul, the genial host, was only a few years older than us, but had already established himself as one of the leading bootleggers in Rockingham County. Paul really was big, six feet, five inches tall and about two hundred and seventy pounds. He had been a terror on the football field in high school. He carried a long-barreled .38 caliber pistol in a shoulder holster. He always claimed he only used it when he had to. I'd never seen him have to, and I didn't want to.

We drove around behind the building and parked. Ralph led the way as we walked to the door. He turned to me just as we reached it. "You want to do the honors?"

"Sure." I reached out and knocked three times slowly, twice quickly, then three more times slowly. An eye appeared at the peephole in the door, then the door swung open. "Hi, Paul." I grinned.

"Well, hello, Charlie, boy. What kind of scum you got with you there? Teddy Hatter. Ralph Dodge. Y'all come on in." The door swung wide and we went into the cabin.

It was decorated like I always thought Hemingway's house would be. There were two deer heads on the wall, and hung above the fireplace two flintlock rifles, crossed. Paul's dad was with the truckers' union, and many of his friends stopped by Paul's for a drink or two after getting in from a run. Sometimes things got a little rowdy, especially during the poker games going on in opposite corners, but all Paul ever had to do was flash that .38 pistol to calm things down again. He was notorious as a dead shot.

We were the only young guys he allowed into his place. He'd let other high school guys come by and buy a bottle or half bottle of liquor, but we were the only ones he let come in and drink. He always let us in, even though we didn't always buy anything, the price of mixed drinks being too expensive for us. Paul said he liked us, and when he liked someone, that was that. Of course, the same was true if he didn't like someone.

Paul leaned against the bar. "What'll you boys have?"

Teddy shrugged. "Nothing for me, Paul. I'm low on funds."

"Me, too," said Ralph.

Paul rubbed his chin. "Aw, hell, boys, have one on the house. It's been a good week." He stepped behind the bar. "Now. What'll it be?"

Teddy leaned forward. "I'll have a gin fizz, please."

"Same for me," said Ralph, leaning beside him.

I walked over and looked at a deer head. "Nothing for me, Paul," I called over my shoulder.

"Didn't you hear me say this one's free?" Paul said, starting to work on Teddy and Ralph's drinks.

"I know. Thank you, Paul. I'm just not in the mood."

"Okay, Charlie. If you say so." He mixed drinks for Ralph and Teddy. They sat at the bar and sipped them, trying to act sophisticated. They ended up laughing and being themselves. I watched them from across the room. Paul had a fire in the fireplace, and I had walked over there, just standing and watching the fire, occasionally glancing over at the others once in a while. After chatting with Teddy and Ralph a bit, Paul came over to where I was.

"Not much business tonight, Paul," I said, looking about the room.

"No. But it's early, yet. Most of the boys don't usually get by here until ten o'clock or later."

"Oh." I stared at the fire.

"What's the matter, Charlie?"

"Nothing."

"You don't act like it's nothing. Out with it, boy."

"It's no big deal, Paul."

"I'll be the judge of that. I'm Eden's biggest man. If it can be handled, I'll handle it. Is it woman trouble again?"

I smiled at the irony. "No."

"School?"

"No. Nothing like that."

"Well, dammit, Charlie, what is it? I'm not Sherlock Holmes."

"Well, Paul, it's like this-" About that time, some customers came knocking. Paul excused himself and went to see to them. He let them in and served them. They came over to the fireplace, laughing and talking with each other. I backed away and went over to the window that faced the road. The lower half was shuttered, but I could look out of the upper half and see the stars. There were thousands of them. I saw one falling and closed my eyes to wish. Someone tapped my shoulder.

It was one of the guys Paul had let in. "Paul wants to see you. Outside."

I thanked him and walked across the room. Before I got halfway to the door, I realized people were watching me. Evidently they'd heard Paul say he wanted to see me outside. I stopped and looked around; most of the faces were disinterestedly serious, like people at an automobile accident when no one they know is involved. I stood there for a minute trying to understand their looks. Then I shrugged and went out.

It was a clear, starry night the last week of October, and with a breeze blowing, chilly. My breath was making vapor and I realized that it was the first night that fall I'd seen it do that. *Winter's coming*, I thought.

I looked around the parking lot. Big Paul was leaning against his car, a red Buick with a huge engine. It was the only car I knew of that would outrun Ralph's 1964 Plymouth Fury at top end. I shivered to fight the chill and walked over to Paul.

"Did I do something wrong, Paul?" I thought uneasily about what the looks I'd gotten might mean. Big Paul was known to be temperamental.

"Naw." He took a drag from a cigarette. "We were just having a private conversation, and I never talk in crowds if I can help it. Somebody might overhear something I didn't want them to know and I'd have to kill them."

"Paul, do you really shoot people and stuff? You speak of it a lot, but do you really do it, or is that to scare people?" It wasn't a very politic question, but I wanted to know.

He took a drag from his cigarette and blew smoky vapor toward the stars. "Well, Charlie," he said, not looking at me, "since you've asked, I'll tell you. I've never killed anybody. I've not even shot anybody. As a matter of fact, I only shot at somebody once, and that was just to scare him. But none of them-" he gestured toward the cabin - 'know that. They think I'll shoot them. And it serves my purposes to let them think that. There are things that you do, Charlie, just to make your life easier."

"Oh." I was unsure how the conversation should go, so I leaned back against the car beside Paul and scuffed my feet in the gravel.

"You were going to tell me about Ralph and Teddy wanting you to help them catch Raoul Lamb." He flipped away his cigarette butt. I watched the glowing end turn over and over, then land on the ground. "Ralph told me all about it while I was mixing their drinks. I knew what was bothering you before I came over to talk to you."

"Paul, do you think what they're wanting to do is right?"

"I think they're going to do it whether it is or not. Charlie, there are some people who are going to try to get revenge for every act they see as a wrong whether direct or indirect. Ralph is like that. I believe you're more like me. You're someone who says 'Live and let live.' As far as I can tell, either way could be right-or wrong. I don't guess it matters much in the long run."

"It matters a whole lot if you're looking at the prospect of being queer bait." I sighed and looked up at the stars.

Paul laughed and slapped me on the shoulder. "Charlie, you're all right. You still write poems for the school newspaper literary page like those you showed me that time?"

I nodded. "Yeah, when they'll print them."

Paul cocked his head like a farmer examining a tobacco leaf. "You know some people would think *you're* a fag because you write poetry, don't you?"

"What?"

He gestured at the cabin. "Tell you what. Go on back in there and tell some of those roughnecks you're a poet."

"No thanks. I get the idea. But why are you telling me this, Paul?"

"To prove a point to you. You're all worked up about what Ralph wants you to do because you've got this idea that acting like queer bait will make you be a queer. It won't. Right, wrong, queer, not queer--all that stuff is just in people's heads. It don't matter unless *you* let it. The best advice I can give you, Charlie, is do what *you* can stand. If going along with Ralph and Teddy on this is going to bug you too much, don't do it. The only thing you can have for sure is peace of mind, Charlie, and getting that can be a full-time job."

I bowed my head and scuffed my shoes on the gravel again. "That's pretty tough-minded, Paul," I said at last. "I don't know if I can be that way. It's my nature, I think, to let things get to me. That's why I write poems. I don't know. I guess I'm crazy to let stuff bother me. Teddy and Ralph don't seem to, as much."

"I believe you're wrong, there, Charlie," Paul said.

"Why?"

"Because people deal with things in different ways. Teddy, for instance, is bothered by a lot of the same things you are. But instead of writing a poem or something, he just goes crazy and does something wild, like with Diana Delight; or else he just laughs it off as if it's a joke. Ralph, he's another way. He takes everything head-on. Like this business with Lamb. Ralph's going right after him, because he feels Lamb's done him wrong. That's his way. And you, of course, write poems or such."

"Charlie, is that you?" Teddy had come out and was standing on the front steps. "You ready to go?"

"Yeah. In a minute." I looked up at the stars once more, then at Paul. "Thanks for the advice."

He lit another cigarette. "No charge, Charlie. Remember, though. Do what you can stand to do. No more."

"Okay. Thanks again, Paul."

"Let's go, Charlie," called Ralph. "It's getting late."

"Be right there." I heard the Plymouth fire up.

"You better hustle," Paul said. "That crazy Ralph might leave you."

I offered my hand and Paul shook it. "Why don't we double date one night, Paul? I know some girls over in Reidsville who'd show you a good time."

He shook his head. "I don't know, Charlie. I'm pretty busy. I usually get only one night a week off, and then I like to take it easy. These girls pretty?"

"Real nice, Paul, real nice. Think about it. You got my phone number?"

"Yeah, I believe so. One other thing, Charlie-"

"Yeah?" We were walking toward Ralph's car.

"With the way you run after women, and the way they run after you, I don't think you've got anything to worry about. Take it from Eden's biggest man."

"Thanks, Paul." I trotted to the Plymouth and Teddy let me into the back seat.

"About time," Ralph said to the rear view mirror as we pulled away.

III

The next afternoon went by as if in a dream. Teddy came by and picked me up about four o'clock. We drove over to Ralph's. When we got there, he had all kinds of preparations made. "Try this on," he said, handing me a sweatshirt.

I slipped the sweatshirt on over my shirt and sweater. It was too tight.

"Take your sweater off," he said impatiently.

"I don't want to. This is the one Paula gave me for my birthday."

"Charlie, Paula broke up with you," Ralph said as if explaining something to a child. "She goes steady with some guy name Ron. She doesn't love you anymore. She probably never did."

"Don't say that, Ralph."

He snorted disgustedly. "Charlie, take the damn sweater off."

"No."

"Good lord, boy. I'll hang it right here in my closet. It'll be as safe as if you had it at home. Safer than *if* you had it on." He held out his hand.

"How do you figure that?" I asked, arms crossed, sullen.

"Well," he groped for a second, "well, you could spill something on it, couldn't you?"

I turned and looked out the window. "Put on the Rolling Stones," I said.

"In a minute. First, take off the sweater."

"No. Teddy, put the Stones on the stereo."

"What do you want to hear?" asked Teddy, thumbing through the record rack. I turned to watch him.

"*Beggar's Banquet*. Play 'No Expectations.'"

Teddy took the record from its jacket and put it on the turntable. Then Ralph waved him off. "Not yet, Teddy. Charlie, please take off the sweater so the sweatshirt will fit."

"I really don't want to, Ralph. Don't you have a bigger sweatshirt?"

"No, I don't. Besides, this one's perfect. I used to wear it when I was in junior high." He was right. It looked like the kind of sweatshirt some twelve-year-old would wear. It was dingy white with irremovable grass stains and a Baltimore Colts emblem on the front. "Ralph, I don't have to do this," I said.

"Yes, you do. You said you would."

"When did I say that?"

"Last night. Just before we got up with those Mayodan girls. Or maybe while we were parking. I don't remember exactly."

"I never said I would. You made that up in your mind, boy."

"Charlie," said Teddy as he put the needle down on the record and Keith Richards' slide guitar droned out of the speakers, "if you don't want to do it, don't. But if we're gonna do it, let's get on with it. We're wasting time here." He reached into the closet and took out Ralph's guitar, a sunburst Gibson hollow body electric with no cutaways. He began strumming along with the record, adjusting the tuning as he saw fit.

I stood looking at them. For Teddy, the whole thing was obviously a lark. Ralph was watching me as if he was a clothing salesman and was waiting to see if I was going to buy the suit or not. I pulled off the sweatshirt. I took off my sweater, folded it carefully, and handed it to Ralph. He put it on a hanger and hung it in his closet. I put the sweatshirt back on. "You want me to change into some jeans or something?" I asked.

Ralph looked me up and down. "No. The sweatshirt will do. Here, carry this." He reached into the closet and brought out an old basketball, one we'd played with on the junior high play ground. "Stand on the corner and dribble this."

"Perfect," Teddy said.

"Well." I took a deep breath and let it out with a whoosh. "Let's do it."

Teddy put the guitar back into the closet. He scooped up his jacket and glided out the door. I turned and followed.

"Charlie?" Ralph said quietly.

I stopped in the doorway and faced him. "Yeah?"

"Thanks for doing this. It means something to me."

"Yeah, I know. I don't mind as much since it's for you, Ralph." He snapped off the stereo and came over and put his arm around my shoulder. We walked down the hall together, Teddy standing at the front door watching us. As we reached him, I pulled away suddenly.

"Watch it, man. You had Raoul on the brain too long or something?" I winked at Teddy who had opened the front door.

"Why, you little"--we dashed across the front yard, Ralph after me like a hound after a fox. As we reached the garage behind the house, he caught me. "I'll teach you, you little-"

"Ralph Dodge, let that boy alone," yelled Quentin Waller, Ralph's next door neighbor. He'd been raking leaves in his yard and had seen us. "I'm going to tell your daddy." He scowled, waggling a finger at Ralph.

Ralph let go of me and faced him. "Tell him. I don't care. He thinks you're crazy, anyway."

Quentin dropped his rake and headed for the house. "I'm going to call the police," he threw over his shoulder.

Ralph turned to us calmly. "Third time this month."

"That proves it," said Teddy, reaching down and scooping up a handful of gravel.

"Proves what?" I asked.

He shrugged as if stating the obvious. "You should never tell crazy people they're crazy. It's too great a shock to their systems."

"I believe you're right, Teddy." I reached down for my own handful of gravel, as did Ralph.

"Ready?" Ralph said.

"Whenever you are, Ralphie, boy." Teddy smiled. "After all, he's your neighbor."

"Don't remind me. One, two, three, go!"

We all hurled gravel at the tin roof of Quentin's house. The gravel made a dreadful noise when they landed on it. We knew from experience.

As Ralph cranked his car, Quentin came thundering out of his house waving the blank gun that he always tried to frighten us with.

"Look at that fool," said Teddy as we backed out of Ralph's drive.

"You know who he reminds me of? I was thinking about it the other night"--Ralph glanced around to see if we were listening"--he reminds me of the old guy in *Huckleberry Finn*. The one who was always feuding? Colonel Grangerford."

Teddy and I looked at each other, surprised. "You really read *Huckleberry Finn*, Ralph?" I said.

"Yeah. I did. In spite of old lady Cedar I read it. I liked Huckleberry. He was real, you know? Like a person."

"Yeah, I know," I said understandingly. "I really like Tom Sawyer that way."

Teddy laughed. "You would, Charlie. You're just like him. If Tom Sawyer were alive today, he'd hang around with you and wear a different alpaca sweater everyday. Just like you."

"I've only got five--or six," I protested.

"Yeah, but you've always got one on." Teddy turned and smiled.

Ralph stepped sharply on the brakes. "Hey, we're about to drive by the DeMolay building."

"You sure this'll work?" I said nervously. The moment of truth was hitting me hard.

"Don't worry, Charlie. Teddy and I have it all planned. Everything will go just fine. Providing Lamb comes by here." Ralph parked the car behind the DeMolay building. I got out of the car and, basketball under my arm, walked up to the corner of Bridge Street and Early Avenue, according to plan. I stood on the corner dribbling the basketball idly. After about ten minutes I got bored, so I started tying to do fancy tricks with the ball. Twice it got away from me and rolled out into Bridge Street. A car almost hit me the second time I ran into the street to fetch the ball. After that, I went and sat on the low stone wall in front of the DeMolay building and tried twirling the ball on my index finger. I didn't have much success. I got so engrossed in twirling, or trying to, that I didn't notice the Chevrolet Bel Air pull up at the curb on Early Avenue.

"Sonny! Hey, sonny! Come here a minute."

I looked over at the car. It was Raoul Lamb. "What do you want?" I asked, looking at him through narrowed eyes.

"Just to talk. Come here a minute."

I got up slowly and walked over to within about a yard of the car. "Yeah?"

"You waiting for someone?"

"Yeah. My--um--sister. I've been playing ball over at the school." Leaksville Elementary School was just across the way.

"Who's your sister?"

"Oh." I needed a name. I acted suspicious to stall. "Why do you want to know?"

"Just curious," he said innocently.

"Umm, Jenny Swan's my sister."

"Jenny Swan. That can't be right. She's my third cousin. Her brother's older than she is. Hey, wait. I know you. You're no kid. You worked at Meadow Dairies last summer." He looked around quickly, nervously. "Is this some kind of trick?"

"Yeah! You bet it is!" It was Teddy. He was trying to get the passenger side door open, but it was locked. Raoul reached for his ignition key. I didn't try to stop him. Suddenly, Ralph was beside me. He grabbed the basketball from me and threw it hard at Raoul's head, right through the open car window, as he started the car. The blow stunned Raoul, and he let out the clutch. His car jumped and died, throwing Teddy, who still had hold of the passenger side door handle, out into Early Avenue. He jumped to his feet cursing. "Dammit, Ralph, my mother will raise hell when she sees this rip! This is my new London Fog jacket!"

Ralph never heard him. He'd jerked open Raoul's car door and grabbed his keys. He turned and threw them up into the yard of the DeMolay building. "Well, well, Raoul," he said, his face a thundercloud, "looks like we're going to have ourselves a little party."

"What--what do you mean?" Raoul asked. He looked scared and almost sick. He was a little guy, slight like me, but shorter. The side of his face was red from where the basketball had hit him.

Ralph turned to me. "Charlie, go across the street to the Quik Pik and get a wide roll of masking tape. Get a magic marker, too."

I trotted across Early Avenue and into the store, moving as if in a cloud. I bought the tape, a marker, and a

Dr. Pepper for myself. As I came out of the store, I looked over toward Raoul's car, which was sitting partway out in Bridge Street. There was a green Pontiac GTO blocking its path. Gary Coverdale's car. I walked over and gave Ralph the tape and marker. It was then, when I'd gotten around on the other side of the cars, that I saw what they'd done to Raoul.

Gary had gotten a piece of rope from his car and they'd tied Raoul's hands with it. They'd taken his belt off and bound his feet with that. He was leaning against a telephone pole and sobbing like a child.

Ralph tore off a piece of tape. He pushed back Raoul's head. Raoul tried to shake him off, but Ralph shoved his head hard against the pole and pressed the tape over his mouth. Teddy handed Ralph a piece of cardboard on which he'd written "QUEER" in large letters with the marker. Ralph taped it to the front of Raoul's shirt. Then Ralph, Teddy, and Gary picked up Raoul and took him out into the middle of the intersection, right under the stoplight. They stood him up out in the middle of the street. Raoul struggled and wiggled and finally fell down. They just laughed and left him lying there. Just as he fell, the streetlights came on. Gary ran and jumped into his car, backed it away from Raoul's, and roared off down Bridge Street. Teddy and Ralph came dashing past me. "Let's go!" shouted Teddy. He leaped up onto the wall where I'd been sitting and ran along it as it went down the side of the DeMolay building. I heard the Plymouth fire up and Ralph's voice calling me.

I looked back toward Bridge Street. Several cars had come to rest, facing each other, on opposite sides of the intersection, Raoul in the middle. Most of them were high school kids, blowing their horns and laughing. One man about forty years old got out of his pickup truck and went over to where Raoul lay on his side. He nudged him with his foot. When Raoul rolled over, the man looked at him, then went back to his truck, got in, and drove carefully around the other cars.

Then I saw a blue '64 Chevy Impala pull over to the side of Bridge Street. Jenny Swan, for some reason wearing her cheerleading outfit, got out of her car and ran over to Raoul. She knelt beside him and pulled the sign off. Then she pulled the tape off his mouth. He called her name and she hugged him. She helped him to sit up and tried to untie his hands. She was having trouble, so she stood up and called for help. "Help, please! Help, somebody!" Everyone got quiet; most backed up their cars and drove away. Then she saw me.

"Charlie! Charlie Beagle! Come, help me, please!" I got up and started to her. Raoul said something. She bent over and listened to him. She stood up and looked at me and I stopped where I was at the curb. She knelt and went back to work on Raoul's hands. I pulled off the sweatshirt and threw it up into the DeMolay yard. I went over and untied Raoul's hands. I helped Jenny to her feet as he untied his own feet. She reached down to help him up; I did the same. He jerked away from me. He said something indistinct to Jenny and walked over to the DeMolay building. In a couple of minutes he had found his keys. He got into his car, started it, called to Jenny again, and then drove slowly away. I took her arm and we walked over to the wall at the DeMolay building, leaving the belt and things just lying in the street. We sat down on the wall and I stared at the sidewalk. She took her fingertips and raised my head until we were looking into each other's eyes.

She shook her head gently. "Oh, Charlie," was all she said.

"I'm sorry." It was so inadequate that I felt stupid; then I started to cry, which made me feel twice as stupid. She pulled me to her and laid my head in her lap. She bent over me, crying herself, and gave me a little kiss on the cheek.

I stopped crying and sat up, wiping my face ferociously. I looked back to where Ralph was parked, but he and Teddy were gone somewhere. I looked at Jenny. She used her fingertips to wipe away a last tear. I felt like puking. Then I got this funny feeling I couldn't put my finger on. It was the same as when in the second grade I'd looked at someone else's paper during a spelling test and got an answer. Nobody had caught me, but whenever I thought about it, I got the same feeling. I knew I'd done something I couldn't make right. I shivered. Jenny put her arms around me and held me, but it didn't make me warm.

I should've listened to Big Paul.

THE CRUSADES

"Let be be finale of seem
The only emperor is the Emperor of Ice Cream."

Wallace Stevens

I

"That took guts." Ralph scanned the wall.

"Evidently," I said, shaking my head.

"Takes a man to make a statement like that," said Ralph, rubbing his hand over the paint on the wall.

"Yeah. It takes a man--or a fool--one or the other." Teddy leaned against the wall and lit a plain end cigarette. He smoked plain ends so other people wouldn't bum smokes off him.

During the night before this particular Friday in this particular week in April, someone had painted on the wall of the smoking area in bright orange "WHITE POWER! BLACK TRASH!"

"All right, boys, let's clear out. Smoking area's closed until further notice." Mr. Paladin, an assistant principal, stood looking down at us from the steps leading into the gym lobby which doubled as a smoking area for students with parental permission. Parental permission consisted of having a friend sign a permission slip in a faintly authoritative hand.

Ralph crushed his cigarette on the side of one of the oil drums half filled with sand and used as ashtrays. Teddy flipped his cigarette at the barrel. It hit the side and bounded away. It lay on the cement floor, smoke curling from it. Teddy bounded up the steps and held the door open for Ralph. I walked over to his cigarette.

Mr. Paladin turned to Teddy. "You want to pick up that cigarette, Mr. Hatter?"

"Not particularly." Teddy went through the doorway after Ralph, letting the door slam behind him.

Mr. Paladin started to call after him, but I spoke up. "I'll get it." I scooped up the smoke and tossed it into the drum. I trudged up the steps past Paladin.

"Charlie?"

"Yes sir?"

"Tell Teddy Hatter I'll see him in my office at 3:20."

"Yes sir." I opened the door and walked through. On impulse I pulled it and let it slam. I glanced back through the chicken wire reinforced window. Paladin was staring. I shrugged and walked down the hall past the cafeteria. I turned left and went out the side door and under the walkway into the classroom building. Ralph was getting his books out of his locker. I went over to him. "Teddy's in it but good this time."

"Paladin?"

"Yeah. Why has he got such a chip on his shoulder today?"

"Diana Delight. She called him last night. You know how she can tear him up inside."

"Yeah, but, hell, she does that about every two-three weeks. He ought to be getting immune by now." I leaned my forehead against the lockers and looked at my loafers. There was a spot on my left shoe, so I spit on my finger and rubbed it off.

"Listen, Charlie." Ralph looked around carefully, then leaned close and whispered, "You heard anything about a riot?"

"A what?" I stood straight up and looked at him as if he were crazy.

"Shh. A riot. As Teddy and I came into the classroom building, Bobby Hilton came by and said the niggers were going to riot today at lunchtime. On account of the smoking area thing."

"Bullshit." I leaned my head against the locker again, but I turned my face toward Ralph. "Mr. Newley said last month, after those guys put that casket with the black mannequin in it in the auditorium, that the next person from either side who did anything to cause trouble would be expelled. Permanently."

"Yeah, but I bet he'll never catch the guys from last night." He spoke in an uneasy tone. I wondered what he knew.

"Newley always catches everybody," I said firmly.

"Not if nobody tells," he whispered, a little shrilly.

"Somebody always tells, Ralph," I said wearily, shaking my head as I straightened up. "People can't seem to help but feel like big shots when they've done something, even something like that. So, they tell some 'friend' and that 'friend' tells someone else, and pretty soon, Newley knows."

Ralph rolled his eyes. "You've got it all figured out, don't you, lover boy?"

I shrugged. "Pretty much. Where did Teddy go?"

"On up to Mrs. Berkeley's room. He's got an English test and he didn't study. Again."

I shook my head again. "I swear, that boy's gonna flunk the twelfth grade." The homeroom bell rang. I turned to go to my locker. Ralph caught my arm.

"You got any protection?" he whispered, looking up and down the hall.

I grinned at him. "No, but there's a machine in the men's room at Martin's Service Station where for twenty-five cents you can buy it in one of four sensuous colors."

"Dammit, Charlie, I mean a weapon. A knife or something in case the niggers try to get smart with us."

I chuckled, but he scowled and continued before I could crack another joke. "Listen," he said, "I got a straight razor here in my pocket. I've also got an old hunting knife in the glove compartment of my car. I'll sneak out there second period and get it for you. I'll put it in your locker."

"Ralph," I said, putting my hand on his shoulder, "I really don't think I'm going to need a *weapon*."

"Why not?"

"Because if a fight as bad as what you're suggesting breaks out I'm going to run like hell."

"You mean you aren't going to help us kill niggers?"

"I mean I don't aim to end up a dead white boy."

Ralph snorted. "Dating Jenny Swan's done made you soft, Charlie."

I patted him on the shoulder. "No, sir. Not at all. Dating Jenny's made me sane." The tardy bell rang. "Good lord, Ralph, I've got to go. I've got Grant for homeroom and she'll raise hell at me."

"Go on, then." I'll still get that knife and put it in your locker. Just in case you need to defend Miss Jenny's honor." He grinned and backed away.

"I won't need it."

"You never can tell." He turned and ran. So did I. As I slid to a stop in front of Mrs. Grant's door, I heard Mr. Newley's voice boom through the classroom building. Ralph had gone out and failed to shut the door.

"Where are you supposed to be, Ralph Dodge?"

II

When homeroom let out, Mrs. Grant kept me for a thirty-second "Be on time" lecture. By the time I got out into the hall, it was full of people, but nobody was making noise to speak of. It must have been like Paladin and Berry, the assistant principals, would have dreamed it. People were talking, but in whispers. I didn't think much about it, just hustled to my locker, grabbed my English book, and headed for first period. Jenny would be there.

As I trotted up the stairs to the second floor where my class was, I got an introduction to what Ralph was talking about. Stephen Varslee, a black guy known around school for his adulation of the Black Panthers, brushed against me as we passed on the stairs. " 'Scuse me,' " I threw over my shoulder. Suddenly a hand whirled me around, and I nearly fell on the stairs.

"Watch it, Honky!" He stood on the step below and glared at me. I looked him up and down. He was holding his books in his right hand, his left clenched in a fist. I wondered if he were left-handed. Traffic on the stairs had stopped. The steps were crowded, and they were all watching us. I checked the crowd. There were about two-thirds white kids, but almost all of the whites were girls, while most of the blacks were guys. Tammy Scarsdale, a cheerleader and friend of Jenny's and mine, tugged the back of my shirt. "Let's go to class, Charlie," she whispered tensely. I looked around at her. She was scared.

I shrugged. "Okay." I turned to follow her.

"Look at the white boy run," sneered Stephen. I couldn't let that pass. I faced him.

"C'mon, Charlie." Tammy tugged my sleeve.

"Tell Mrs. Raker I might be a minute late," I said to her, loudly enough for everyone to hear.

"A *minute*," scoffed Stephen, looking around for support. A voice called out, "Get him, blood!"

"You run on, Tammy," I said loudly. *"This won't take long."* The second part came out through clenched teeth. I slid my books in front of me so he couldn't kick me. I considered him. He was taller than me, but thinner. I was slender, but Stephen was downright skinny. "Muhammad Ali and Jerry Quarry," I murmured aloud.

"What you saying, *boy*?"

I looked at him; he was tensed like a cat. *What the hell*, I thought. I said, " 'Muhammed Ali and Jerry Quarry.' That's us, right?"

There was a snicker in the crowd. Then someone laughed out loud. The laughter spread until it was general. Stephen stared around at everyone. I turned and went up the stairs. "Hey, come back here," Stephen called.

"Sorry, man, I got a class."

"Then I'll see you at lunchtime, *boy*."

"Not if you go blind." I got another laugh. People were moving again. I raced down the hall, eased open Mrs. Raker's door, and slipped into her room. Luckily, my seat was against the near wall, only the second one in the row, between Tammy and Jenny.

"What happened?" whispered Tammy, twisting in her seat.

" 'It was the best of times, it was the worst of times,' " read Mrs. Raker aloud.

"The first page of *A Tale of Two Cities*," Jenny whispered.

"I know. Thanks." I smiled at her.

"What happened?" Tammy asked again.

"I turned the whole thing into a joke." I leaned toward her.

"How?"

"I made this joke about Muhammad Ali and Jerry Quarry."

"About *what*?" they both whispered.

"Muhammad Ali and Jerry Quarry," I explained patiently. "They're famous boxers."

"Oh." They obviously didn't see the humor.

I shrugged. "I'll explain later."

The whole time Mrs. Raker had been reading the first page of *A Tale of Two Cities*. Just as Jenny, Tammy, and I finished our conversation, she posed a question to the class. "Would anyone like to articulate his or her ideas about the famous opening of Dickens's novel?"

I casually let my gaze wander over the room. When my eyes reached the front, I realized that Mrs. Raker was looking pointedly at our row. There were only the three of us in that row.

"Um, Mrs. Raker"--Tammy said, scrambling in her notes, "I think it means-"

"Mrs. Raker"--Jenny frantically waved her hand beside my face-"I think it means-"

"Never mind, ladies," I said, waving my hands theatrically to quiet them. "I'll answer this."

"Yes, Charles." Mrs. Raker took her glasses off and held them on the corner of her podium for a moment. "Why don't *you* tell us what this paragraph means?" She put her glasses back on, closed her book, and leaned on her podium, hands clasped, waiting.

I looked back and forth at Tammy and Jenny. They were looking at me trustingly. I looked at the rest of the class. Jeff Pound was smiling that same knowing smile we always traded whenever either of us answered in class. It was our way of letting each other know that we knew that we were the ones who *really* understood literature. I looked past him, out the window at the treetops, just covered with tiny leaves, and began. "What Dickens means, or at least what *I think* he means-" Mrs. Raker smiled, acknowledging my attempt at modesty, "by all this 'best of times, worst of times' and 'epoch of uncertainty, epoch of certainty' stuff-"

"Mrs. Raker, I have a question." Jenny waved her hand again.

"Jenny, an epoch is a period of time," I said grandly, anticipating her question. She shook her head as if I hadn't answered what she wanted. I raised my eyebrows and continued. "Anyway, what he's after is that the time presented in *A Tale of Two Cities* is much like our own. Things were happening that people could interpret in a multiplicity of ways." I saw Mrs. Raker smile again, and knew she'd caught my use of a vocabulary word from the previous week.

I looked around the room. Some people were nodding their heads in agreement, some were leaning on their arms trying to look like they were thinking, others were playing with their pencils or doodling on paper, passing the time until class ended. I leaned back in my seat self-satisfiedly.

"Name a few of these events that people were interpreting in this-what was it?" Mrs. Raker asked sweetly.

"*Multiplicity* of ways," Jeff Pound deadpanned.

"Yes. The events, Charles?" Her voice had ice in it."

"Ah. Well, um-" I fumbled.

"There were several," said Jenny quietly. "The French Revolution, obviously. The Reign of Terror, although I suppose that's part of the French Revolution. The war between England and France. The rise of Romanticism. Those were a few of the things going on then." She patted my shoulder.

I took the note she passed me. I read it and smiled. She'd asked if I had to wash my hair that night, since it was Friday. I turned to her and shook my head. I wrote "Greensboro?" under her note, refolded it and passed it back over my right shoulder, acting as if I was scratching my head. "Charlie, Mrs. Raker's talking to you," she whispered. I hadn't been paying attention.

"Yes ma'am?" I said, looking up, surprised.

"I was saying, *Charles*, that *your* explanation of the opening of Dickens' novel would have been much stronger had you, as Jenny did, named some of the important events that specifically reflect what Dickens was referring to."

"Yes, ma'am."

"Very well. Now, let's go on with the rest of the first section of the novel." Mrs. Raker put her glasses back on.

We spent the rest of first period talking about *A Tale of Two Cities*. I kept trying to get a minute to talk to Jenny, but Mrs. Raker asked me questions whenever I tried to turn in my seat. Finally the bell rang to end class. As we walked into the hall, I asked Jenny if she wanted to go to Greensboro to a restaurant and a movie. I'd gotten my income tax refund from my summer job and was loaded.

"Let's just stay in town, tonight." She said shyly. "We could go to the seven o'clock show at the Grand Theatre. They've got *Romeo and Juliet* on."

"But that'll be over at nine," I said as we walked along, "what'll we do then?" I had hopes, but I dared not voice them. I'd never been able to work up the nerve to take Jenny parking, though we'd been dating fairly steadily (steady for me; she still saw her ex-steady twice a month when he was home from the University of North Carolina) for two months, and going out with some regularity for three (since the Raoul Lamb thing).

She looked at me, her eyes sparkling blue. "My parents are going out of town for a building contractor's convention in Charlotte this weekend. They'll leave today about noon. I thought maybe--if you liked--we could go to my house for the rest of the evening. My grandmother will be there, but she never comes out of her room after nine o'clock." She blushed.

"Sure. That'll be fine," I said, trying to keep my voice from cracking. "I'll see you later, then." I started down the hall away from her.

"Charlie?" she called lightly.

"Yeah?"

"Since we're both going to the same class, don't you think we could walk together?"

"Oh. Yeah. I guess we could."

I was in heaven.

III

The first part of second period went smoothly enough. Miss Slater was absent; so French III had a forty-five minute assignment that I completed in about twenty. The rest of the time I would have spent fooling around, making eyes at Jenny, had the substitute teacher not sent me down to the language lab. I went down there, let myself in, and hooked up tape 26. Tape 26 was supposed to be about Dominique and Henri, the children of a Norman fisherman who lived in Dinard, France. Instead, tape 26 was Jimi Hendrix, Jefferson Airplane, and the Beatles. Ralph and I had gotten one of Miss Slater's blank tapes, recorded our own tape, and switched it for the real tape 26. We were careful to use 26 only when we were working with one of the individual tape recorders. If we'd played it on one of the players hooked to the control console, Miss Slater could've found us out by flipping a switch. The first time I ever used tape 26, Miss Slater asked me how I liked the information on Normandy. I told her it was music to my ears. Ralph just about gagged when I told him that later.

Anyway, I was down in the language lab enlightening myself to a little Jefferson Airplane when I vaguely heard the door click. I looked up to see Mr. Newley coming into the lab. I switched off the tape, lowered the headphones, and greeted him. "Um, hello, sir. Miss--the sub--she sent me down here to listen to a tape because I finished my assignment early."

"I know, Charlie. I came here from Miss Slater's room. I want to talk with you about something that happened this morning."

I thought fast. "Oh, well, if Mr. Paladin is upset about that door slamming this morning, that was an accident."

He looked at me strangely, then for a moment I thought he was going to smile. "No," he said, rubbing his chin, "that's not what I wanted to speak to you about. I understand you almost had a fight with Stephen Varslee this morning."

I raised my eyebrows, surprised. So someone had gone to Newley about that. I ran over in my memory the people on the stairs this morning trying to recall someone who would go to Newley. I came up empty. "Well, Mr. Newley," I said, "I guess it wasn't really a fight. Stephen likes to run his mouth, you know, and I guess tempers are running high in the black community right now."

Mr. Newley gave me a look that told me I'd made a profound understatement.

"What happened was, I was hurrying up the stairs to the second floor for my first period class and I brushed against Stephen. I said 'excuse me,' but that wasn't good enough for him. He wanted to make a big scene. Then I got to thinking about us fighting, and it seemed pretty silly to me, so I said 'Muhammad Ali and Jerry Quarry.' That got everybody laughing, and I was able to get away from him without a fight. That's all there was to it." I fiddled with my headphones.

Mr. Newley nodded. He put his hands in his pants pockets and began rocking back and forth from heel to toe. "Do you think there'll be any more trouble between you and Stephen, Charlie?"

"Not really. Like I said, Stephen is usually mouthy."

"I understand. Well, if he says anything else to you, come straight to me. I'll see you." He turned on his heel and was gone.

I rolled my chair around to look after his retreating form. Mr. Newley's last comment bothered me a bit. I took off the headphones and put them on the tape player. "Mr. Newley," I called. I heard his slow tread stop, then return. He stuck his head in the doorway. "You don't think there'll be any more trouble today, do you, Mr. Newley?" I asked.

He shook his head ruefully. "I don't know, Charlie. There's some ugly talk going on around this school today.

Stupid stunts like that business last night in the smoking area are too much for some people to accept, I'm afraid."

He disappeared before I could think of anything else to say. I sat back in my rolling chair and tried to get my bearings. I tried to figure out how I'd feel if the words 'black' and 'white' had been reversed on the slogan in the smoking area. I don't know how long I sat there, but I must have been concentrating hard because I didn't hear Jenny come in. I only heard her when she called softly, "Charlie? Are you asleep?"

I looked up. She had the door closed, and she was holding the doorknob in her hands behind her. I smiled at her. She smiled back. I wished I was handsome or bold or both so I would get up and go kiss her or something equally Hollywood. "Hi," I said. "I had my head bent over, thinking. Sometimes I close my eyes because it helps me concentrate.

Jenny tilted her head like the RCA dog and looked at me. "You think a lot, don't you, Charlie?"

I sighed. "Yeah. Probably too much."

She came over and knelt beside my chair. She sat back on her calves like in her cheerleading picture, except she didn't have on her cheerleading outfit. I leaned forward and put my chin in my hands.

"Thinking again?" she said teasingly.

I turned and studied her face with the slow gaze I use when I'm trying to understand something like a painting. Her hair was very black, with sheen like silver, and it was parted in the middle and hung in gentle curves that reached her shoulders. Her skin was fair, but not overly fair so that she looked pale or unhealthy. She had the peaches and cream look, with only the cream, no peaches. Her eyes were a deep blue, sort of like the sky at twilight on a clear day when the blue deepens until it becomes violet. Her eyes were the blue just before the violet. I smiled again, this time without showing any teeth.

"You smile like that when you make a wrong answer in English class, Charlie. What kind of smile is it?"

"It's the smile of a guy who knows he's licked. You're the most beautiful girl I've ever known, Jenny."

She tilted her head and gave me a questioning look. "More beautiful than Paula?"

I dropped my head. Jenny's question made me confront my perception of the two girls. Paula was tall, green-eyed and naturally blonde, a beauty in her own right. Most people though would have thought Jenny more beautiful. I didn't, and in doing so made a disturbing discovery about my feelings for her. "No," I said, not looking at her, "not more beautiful than Paula."

"Oh, Charlie," she said. Her voice tone took me right back to that night on the wall beside the DeMolay building. I knew I'd failed her again. "I didn't mean to be catty," she whispered.

"I know." I sighed. I looked at her earnestly. "You were always-sort of-a dream, Jenny. I never expected to be going out with someone like you. I'm even-you know-a little afraid." I was surprised at myself for saying all that.

She smiled, a gentle, forgiving smile. "I didn't expect to be going out with you, either, Charlie."

"No doubt."

"But not for the reason you think. You're really smart, Charlie. That scares me, I guess."

"What? Hell, girl, you're valedictorian."

She smiled again. "Only because someone like you or Jeff Pound doesn't want to be, Charlie. I'm a good student. You're smart. There's a difference. You're the first boy I've ever kept dating knowing he was smarter than me."

I didn't know what to say, so I kept my mouth shut. The bell rang ending second period. I turned to the tape player and began rewinding 26. Jenny came over and leaned back against the table where I was working. "You have study hall next period, don't you, Charlie?"

"Yep. But I can't go the library. Mr. Bane caught Teddy and me down on the baseball field working on double plays last week when we were supposed to be doing research."

She wrinkled her perfect brow. "Would he let you out if another teacher asked for you?"

I scratched my head. "Maybe. But I don't know how I'll get any other teacher, even Mrs. Raker, to give me a pass so I can get out of class for no good reason."

"Coach Kendall might," she said.

"Yeah, he might. It might snow in July in North Carolina. But I ain't betting on it." I stood and replaced the tape on the shelf above the table.

"He might give you a pass if *I* asked him to." I looked at her smiling and could almost see Coach Kendall wrapping around her little finger. I walked to the door and opened it for her, bowing and motioning her through. As she walked through the door she kissed me on the cheek. "Thanks," she whispered.

"Don't thank me," I said. "I'm in the same boat as Kendall."

"How's that, Charlie?" She looked at me, slightly puzzled.

I grinned slyly. "I'm a sucker for a pretty face, too."

"Oh, you're impossible-" She made a grab at me, but I dashed away. I went sliding into French class and grabbed my books. I tossed the key to the language lab (which I'd forgotten to lock, I realized) onto Miss Slater's desk and raced out, the substitute calling after me that she was going to put Jenny and me into her report for being alone together in the language lab the last ten minutes of class.

"Fine," I yelled over my shoulder as I roared down the hall.

"Fine! Fine! Just what were you two doing down there?"

I stopped at the door leading out of the classroom building. I looked back. She was standing in the middle of the hall with her hands on her hips. She was trying to look commanding, but at five feet tall she just looked silly.

"We were speaking French," I told her calmly.

"French! I'll bet you were." By this time two or three other teachers had their heads stuck out of their doors. I couldn't resist the audience.

"Mais oui, Mademoiselle. Le francais, c'est la langue de l'amour, n'est-ce pas?"

She waggled her finger at me. I laughed and pushed open the door. Just as she began to get a couple of words out, the door slammed shut and I couldn't hear her. It wouldn't be important until Monday, anyway.

IV

I ran through the walkway, jerked open the door to the main building, and tore down the side hall past the cafeteria. I slid out into the main hall and started digging for the stairs at the far end next to the front doors of the school. Just as I cut in the afterburners, Mrs. Bane, the Spanish teacher (and Mr. Bane's wife) stepped into the hall directly in front of me. I managed to avoid hitting her head-on, but I brushed her so closely I whirled her around. I kept going, though I knew there was no use.

"Come back here, you!" she called. "Who are you? Come back here, right now."

I chugged to a stop. I shuffled slowly back.

"What is your name, young man?" she spat. Boy, she was mad.

"Charlie Beagle, ma'am."

"Charlie what?"

"Charlie Beagle." The tardy bell rang. I was late for her husband's class.

"Charlie Beagle. Oh, yes, Mr. Bane's spoken of you. He's told me about *you*." That boded ill.

"Yes ma'am."

"Well, what do you have to say for yourself?"

I took a deep breath. "I'm very sorry I was running in the hall. If I'd started to class on time, it wouldn't have been necessary to run. I'm totally in the wrong, and I will never do such a thing again as long as I live." I couldn't help it. It was such a stupid question.

"You don't sound very sincere," she said icily.

"Oh, I'm sincere, Mrs. Bane. I'm so sincere, I may bust open from sincerity."

"Well! For that little smarty-pants remark, you may spend thirty minutes in detention hall Monday afternoon."

I couldn't believe she'd said smarty-pants. I didn't mean to get into more trouble, but "smarty-pants" made me laugh. I tried to hold it in and it came out as a snicker.

"Since you find thirty minutes detention amusing, young man, I'm sure you'll find sixty hilarious."

I quit laughing. "Yes ma'am." I hung my head.

"You may go. I have a class to teach, and I'm sure you have one to attend."

"Yes ma'am." I started away. I turned back just as she was opening the door to her room. "Mrs. Bane, ma'am?"

"Yes?" She seemed surprised I'd approach her again.

"Do you think you could give me a note so my third period teacher won't get mad at me?" I'm one of those people who never seem to learn.

"Certainly not!" She whisked through her doorway and shut the door vigorously.

Maybe if I'd apologized. I turned up the hall and trudged toward the stairs. There was sure to be hell to pay when I got to her husband's room. *At least another thirty minutes from her old man,* I thought. *That means it'll be after five o'clock when I get home. There's no way I can keep Mother from finding out then. When she does, she'll tell Dad, and he'll take my driving privileges for next weekend-*I turned the corner-*so that means no date with Jenny next weekend.* Something else popped into my mind. "Smarty-pants," I murmured. I got tickled again and started laughing. I was snickering again as I climbed the stairs. I tried to calm myself as I went down the hall. I opened the door to Mr. Bane's room and tried to let myself in as quietly as possible.

"So. The prodigal returns," he said sarcastically, from behind the newspaper he appeared to be reading.

"Good morning, sir."

"Good morning, Charlie. I trust you had a leisurely stroll to class."

A whole family of comedians, I thought. "Um, I was-talking to Mrs. Bane. She stopped me in the hall. She didn't give me a note. She said you wouldn't mind."

"Mrs. Bane?" he eyed me narrowly.

"Yes sir."

"Well, that's easy enough to check. I don't suppose you'd try to tell me a tale and use my own wife as an alibi. You wouldn't try that, would you, Charlie?"

"Mr. Bane, I'm supposed to be smart, remember?"

He still looked suspiciously at me. Then he cleared his throat. "So you are. Well, we'll let it go this time."

"Thank you, sir." As I walked to my seat I said to myself, "Well, smarty-pants, there's thirty minutes' detention saved-and probably your weekend, too."

As I got to my seat, there was a knock on the door. Since I was still standing, I went and answered it. It was Jenny. She smiled at me and went over to Mr. Bane. He read the note she handed him, looked at me suspiciously again, and handed the note back to Jenny. "All right, Jennifer. You can have him. Charlie, behave yourself."

"Yes sir." I got my books and followed Jenny into the hall. She closed the door, looked up and down the hall, and then kissed me on the cheek.

"Oh, Charlie," she said. She took my arm and we walked down the hall.

"Is that all you wanted to talk to me about?" I asked facetiously.

"No. I'm not sure what we need to talk about." She sighed and turned loose my arm. I got a sinking feeling.

"Well," I said, "we'll never know until you say what's on your mind."

"Oh, Charlie." She took my arm again and leaned her head on my shoulder.

"We'd gotten that far." We reached the bottom of the stairs. I took her hand and we went down the first side hall to Coach Kendall's room. His door was open. I stepped inside and put my books on a table near his desk.

What are you doing, Charlie?" Kendall came to the door as I slipped out.

I held up my hands innocently. "I'm with Jenny, Coach. Per your instructions."

"Hi, Coach." She smiled her most melting smile and Kendall grinned like a chimpanzee.

"Jenny, you keep this clown straight if you can." He jerked his head at me. "He gives you any trouble, you let me know."

"Oh, don't worry, Coach. Charlie's gentle as a lamb." She led me down the hall away from Kendall who stood in his doorway wearing a bemused expression.

We went out a side door at the end of the hall and down the hill past the auditorium to the football stadium. Jenny led the way around the rim, and we ended up sitting on the hillside behind the visitors' side. "Wouldn't you rather sit on the bleachers?" I asked.

"No," she said, staring into the distance, "I'd like to sit here in the sun where no one can see us."

We walked down the hill a bit and sat down. Jenny leaned back on her hands, drawing her knees up and holding herself up to the sunlight. She shook back her hair to let the sun warm her face. I was sitting to her right, about a foot away. After a few minutes the sun made me feel sleepy, so I lay back in the grass. I plucked a blade of grass and put it into my mouth. I put my hands behind my head and studied the clear blue sky.

Then I got one of my crazy notions. "You know, Becky," I said, "if old Huck were here this'd be about perfect."

I looked over at her. She didn't respond. Her eyes were closed, and for a moment I thought she hadn't heard me. Then she rolled over onto her stomach. She folded her arms for a pillow and laid her head on them watching me. "Tom," she deadpanned, "you don't think Injun Joe could sneak up on us out here, do you?"

"If'n he does, I guess I can handle him." I took the piece of grass out of my mouth and looked at her.

"Oh, Tom, would you protect me?" She leaned her face right over mine, only a couple of inches away.

" 'Course I would-Jenny." I put my arms around her and we kissed. I felt like I was touching an electric fence. Then she laid her head on my chest just under my chin. We lay like that for a while, and then she raised up and looked at me again. "Oh, Charlie," she sighed. "You're exactly who I ought to love."

"But I'm not John Wales. Right?" Her Carolina boyfriend.

She sat up and looked away. "That's not it, exactly."

I sat up with a start. "Sure, it is." I felt myself wanting to get squeaky-voiced, but I fought it. "I'm not John Wales, and you're not Paula Chamblee. We have to admit that. Out loud. To each other. If we don't, we won't ever be anything to each other. You'd always be looking for John in me, and I'd be looking for Paula in you. And we'd end up unhappy, finally, because we'd feel tricked somehow, when it was only our own selfish dreaming fooling us."

She stared hard at me through the last part of that speech, but by that time I was so fired up that talking to her directly wasn't even in my mind. My mother's always told me I don't talk to people, only at them sometimes. "You know, Charlie, that's really insightful." She smiled, a little sadly. "See? You are so smart."

"Aw, I was just talking out of my head. I do that occasionally." I looked at the ground. I couldn't look at her.

She leaned back on her calves and looked around. "It's a lovely day, isn't it?"

"Yes, ma'am."

She turned to me suddenly. "What time are you picking me up tonight, Charlie?"

Framed against the sky as I looked up the hill at her, she reminded me of the Mona Lisa, my favorite painting. My father says I'm girl crazy. "Six- thirty okay?"

"Just fine." She stood gracefully and held out her hands to me. I got to my feet and stood just up the hill from her. Against the green background of the grassy hill, she was Jenny. I'd known her for years. I reached out my hand to her and we climbed the hill together. John Anderson, my jo.

V

Instead of going back into the main building, Jenny and I took a short cut between the main building and the classroom building (through the area where the coal for the boiler was piled, to Jenny's dismay) in order to get to the lunchroom early so as to be at the front of the line. We stepped into the breezeway between the main and classroom buildings just as the bell for lunch rang. People came streaming down the halls and into the lunchroom. Lines formed quickly. Jenny and I wound up at the end of a long line on the right side of the cafeteria. I caught sight of Ralph, Teddy, Bobby Hilton and several other guys in the line going down the left side. I waved to them cheerily. Teddy and Ralph looked at us, then at each other, shook their heads, though smiling good-naturedly, and turned back to the serious harangue Bobby Hilton seemed to be pouring forth.

About that time Stephen Varslee and some other black guys came roaring into the cafeteria. I heard him holler "You're mine, Honky!" Then all hell broke loose. Somebody, maybe Bobby Hilton, grabbed a chair and threw it at the black guys. It hit Orlando Henry on the arm. He jumped away and cursed. The other black guys made for Hilton, Teddy, Ralph, and their group. Varslee kept making for me. I tensed as he closed in, clenching my fists and getting ready to fight. Suddenly Steve Parkland, a friend from English class and the baseball team, left his place in the line and cut off Stephen a few feet from me. He turned to me. "Get Jenny out of here, Charlie."

"Steve-" I took a step toward him. A clatter of chairs came from the other side of the room; people began running for the exits. I caught glimpses of Ralph punching Anthony Regis and Teddy getting hit on the shoulder by Ashmore Stanton.

"Charlie, let's go! Please!" Jenny pulled my arm desperately.

Stephen took a swing at Steve Parkland. Parkland knocked it aside and caught Stephen straight in the face with his fist. I shuddered. Jenny tugged at me again, and I let her lead me out.

We got outside somehow, pushing through the crowd at the door, Jenny leading. She led the way as we went back through the coal storage area and down the hill past the auditorium. Jenny kept going faster and faster. As we got past the auditorium, she let go of my hand and began running. She got a good fifty feet ahead of me. She let herself in at the stadium gate. By the time I got to the gate, she was disappearing into the little group of trees in the far corner of the stadium enclosure.

I couldn't figure why she'd run away. I stopped at the gate. I kept thinking about Teddy and Ralph. I couldn't decide whether to follow her or to go back and try to help them.

"Aw, Jenny," I muttered. I let myself in at the gate and jogged over to the patch of trees. Jenny was sitting in the grass leaning against a sapling. She was pulling clovers from a patch near her hand.

"I haven't found any with four leaves," she whispered so softly I could barely hear her.

I came closer and knelt by her. She kept pulling clovers, looking at them, then discarding them. "I can't find one with four leaves," she whispered again. She bent over near the clover and I thought she might be crying.

"Jenny, are you afraid?" I asked. She looked up. She wasn't crying. I half expect life to be like a book or movie. It never is.

"No, Charlie." I waited for more but no more came.

I didn't know what to say next. I wanted to ask why she'd taken off running, but she hadn't made any sense up to this point, so I figured she probably wouldn't. "Let's go get some lunch," I said cheerfully.

"No," she said solemnly, "I think I'll just sit here until time for class." She was talking with her head down again, and I only half understood.

"What? I'm sorry, Jenny, but I can't hear you when you have your head down like that."

She looked up sharply. "I'll stay here," she said firmly.

"Oh." A pause. "Oh. Well, I'll see you fifth period." I got up and walked up toward the gate.

"Charlie!" I turned at the edge of the trees and looked back. "Bon Appetit!" she called. She smiled and waved. It looked from where I was, though, like her eyes were shiny, as if she'd started to cry. I got to the gate, wondering if I'd done something to make her upset. Then I got to wondering about Ralph and Teddy. I heard sirens coming toward the school. I figured they were in big trouble by now. Instead of leaving the stadium, I went down and sat on the hillside above the field house at the opposite end of the stadium to think for a while. I heard the lunch bell ring and knew that I should go to fifth period. As I walked up the hill there were cars and buses streaming down the road away from school. I was almost afraid to go up to the school. I kept thinking about Ralph and his knives.

Instead of going through the coal yard, I went in the side door of the main building so I could stop by Kendall's room and get my books. When I got there, though, the door was locked. The school was silent. I made my way down the main hall. I didn't notice the state policemen until I was nearly to the cafeteria doors. They were guarding the doors dressed in helmets rather than their standard Smokey the Bear hats. I had the feeling I'd definitely missed something big.

It was then I realized how eerie everything was. Usually at this time of day, at the end of the first lunch and beginning of second, the noise would be at its peak and Newley, Paladin, and Berry would be hurrying everywhere trying to quiet things down. But it was silent.

I could even hear my clothes rustle as I put my hands in my pockets. I leaned back and looked down the side hall. There were state troopers standing at the side entrance to the cafeteria where Jenny and I had been earlier. I looked back at the policemen nearest me. They were eyeing me, but they seemed calm enough. I decided that the worst they could do was run me off. "What happened?" I asked.

"School's out, son. Go home." The trooper's tone was even but firm.

"We must've had some kind of fight, huh?" I walked over to the doors and tried to look in. The troopers stood back against it to block my view. It was then that I noticed that the glass in the doors was knocked out. "Wow." I whistled softly.

"Go on home, now, boy. We don't have time for curiosity seekers."

"Um, listen. I write for the school newspaper. Maybe I could interview you for a story." I fumbled in my pockets for a pencil.

The bigger of the two policemen grabbed my arm fiercely. "Now, son, we've been indulgent with you. If you don't get on from here, we're going to take you to the station like the others."

"Others? What others?" I strained to look through the doors again.

"Okay, kid, that's it." He started down the hall with me toward the smoking area and the back exit.

"Wait, listen, I'll go on, I'm just curious, you know? I mean, gosh, look, I'm sorry, can't you let it pass this time?" I was scared to death.

"You were warned, son." He swung open the door to the smoking area and pulled me through.

"Charlie Beagle!" We stopped.

"Yes sir?"

"You can let him go, Don."

"You sure, Mr. Newley?" The trooper looked hard at me.

"I'm sure."

The trooper turned me toward him roughly. "Don't let me see you around here again, today." He let me go and I stepped through the door gingerly, careful not to touch him. He turned on his heel and stalked away, his boots clicking on the tile floor. The door slammed in my face.

"Come down here, Charlie," Mr. Newley called wearily.

"Yes sir." I walked down the steps, taking them one at a time like a small child. I went over to Mr. Newley with my hands in my pockets, head down. "How's it going, Mr. Newley?" I asked stupidly.

He sighed. "I'm weary, Charlie. Very weary. We've had a mess here today."

"What happened, sir?"

"What happened? I'm not sure. Maybe someone made reference to that nonsense"--he gestured toward the partially cleaned away "White power/Black trash" sign"--maybe, as a couple of people have claimed, a Negro boy tried to get fresh with a white girl, maybe they just started throwing chairs, maybe"--he looked at me intently--"Stephen Varslee started it." He looked around, then back at me. "Maybe, Charlie, people are just as stupid and crazy as I think they are right now."

"Yes sir." I thought about Steve Parkland stepping between Varslee and me.

"Do you know anything about all this, Charlie?" Newley looked hard at me.

"Me? No sir." He knew I was lying.

"Maybe I should call Trooper Jones. He can probably get some answers."

"Mr. Newley, I don't really know anything except some talk that was going around this morning."

"Who was talking?" His voice was a knife.

I wasn't about to play dumb. "Bobby Hilton."

"Who else?"

"I don't know." He looked up toward where the troopers were, then back at me. I got the message.

"Ralph." I felt like Judas.

"Both of those boys were arrested."

"Arrested?" I gave a low whistle.

"Well, taken to the police station. A bunch of fools. Someone could've been badly hurt."

In spite of myself, I asked, "Who all got taken in?"

He shook his head at me. "Who all?"

"Please, Mr. Newley, I'd really like to know."

He considered me a moment. "Charlie, You're a loyal friend," he said quietly. "Let's see, who all got taken in? Bobby Hilton, Ralph Dodge, Teddy Hatter, Steve Parkland, Anthony Regis, Stephen Varslee, Orlando Henry, Ashmore Stanton, one or two more. You know, Charlie, some of those boys had knives-"

"Yes sir." I took off running. I went out the back exit, around the automotive shop and back behind the buildings to the student parking lot beside the auditorium. I jumped into my old Chevelle and took off for the police station. I ran a red light, but I guess there weren't any police around.

VI

I had to park up the hill from the police station. I got in through a side door I knew about because my dad had served jury duty in the courthouse upstairs from the police station. I went to the main desk. "Where are the guys from Morehead High?" I asked.

The officer looked up at me and sneered. "You their lawyer?"

"Yeah, I'm F. Lee Bailey. Where are they? Can I see them?"

"Watch your smart mouth, boy." The officer stood and pulled his gun belt up on his bulging stomach.

"Excuse me, sir. Oh, please, sir, where are they, sir?"

He pointed to a room labeled "Conference." "Right in there. But you can't go in unless you're kin." He sat down again and resumed looking at his magazine.

I went to the door. "Oh, I'm kin," I said, opening it.

"To who?" he cried, jumping up.

"Stephen Varslee." I shut the door behind me.

When I looked around the room, it was a pretty sorry sight. All the black guys were sitting on chairs on one side of the room; all the white guys were on the other side. The cop opened the door, looked at me, then at them, waved his hand disgustedly, and let me stay. I went over and leaned against the long table in the center of the room dividing the groups. Teddy was sitting on the end nearest me. His shirt was torn badly. Every one of them had torn clothes, scratches, or worse. Bobby Hilton was developing a shiner. Steve Parkland was holding a wet, bloody handkerchief to his nose. Among the black guys, Varslee had a handkerchief like Parkland's. I think Ashmore Stanton was getting a shiner, too, but I couldn't tell as well with him. I turned back to Teddy.

"Y'all must've had a blast," I said sarcastically.

"Yeah, it was fun as hell," he replied sullenly.

"I bet it was," I said. "Lose any teeth?"

Several from both sides laughed. "Naw," said Teddy. He looked at me and I saw he was going to have a shiner, too. "Where were you?" he asked.

They all looked at me. I looked at one side, then the other. "I went out with Jenny Swan. We were down at the stadium."

They all looked away or at the ground except Steve Parkland. "She get out okay?" he asked.

"Yeah." His interest in Jenny bothered me.

Teddy took out his wallet and gave Ralph a dollar. "You were right," he said.

"Y'all going to get expelled?" I asked.

Ralph fingered his jaw, which looked red and tender. "Suspended. Probably for a week, though. At least that's what the cop says."

"They gonna keep you here overnight?" I looked around and shivered.

"Naw, just until they talk to our folks," said Parkland through his handkerchief.

Ralph caught my eye. "You really missed it, Charlie."

"Yeah," said Orlando from the other side, "it was like-like- what, bro?" He turned to Anthony, a member of the National Honor Society.

"The Crusades," he said sarcastically, his eyes fixed on the opposite wall.

Ralph leaned back, stuck his feet out and looked at the black guys. "Yeah, it was, kinda."

The cop stuck his head in the door and pointed at me. "Okay, you, out. They're ready to bring the parents down here. Justice Sims has been talking to them upstairs."

"One question before I go, fellas." They all looked up at me.

"What?" asked Bobby.

"Who were the Infidels?"

I slipped out the door before anyone could think of an answer.

VII

The rest of the weekend was a semi-disaster. I went home and faced the Mom-Dad Inquisition for about two hours. I was late picking up Jenny for our date, and things went downhill from there. I kept trying to talk to her during *Romeo and Juliet*, and she finally got mad and told me to shut up. Then I got mad and refused to go in when we got to her house. She didn't even kiss me goodnight. I tried to call her Saturday and Sunday, but she never was home, or so her grandmother said. I heard she went out with Steve Parkland Sunday night.

I got to school late Monday because I'd had a dental appointment. My teeth were still hurting from the dental assistant cleaning them as I tiptoed down the hall to my locker. I opened the door gently and Ralph's hunting knife fell out onto the floor and made a big racket. I stared at it stupidly for a moment. A door opened down the hall and I came to my senses, snatched up the knife, and hid it behind some books. Miss Slater strolled leisurely down to my locker.

"Bonjour, Jean-Paul," she said icily.

I resigned myself to the flames. "Good morning, Mademoiselle."

"I believe you owe me a little detention time, n'est-ce pas? Let's try, say, two hours, one half-hour each day for the next four days, today through Thursday. Detention is in my room this week. Doesn't that sound fine?"

"Yes ma'am. Wonderful." I started to get my books out. Miss Slater checked my books and let me go. As I went down the hall to the stairs, she spoke again.

"C'est la vie, n'est-ce pas, Monsieur?"

I turned to her and smiled my wrong-answer-in-English-class smile. "Non, Mademoiselle. C'est la guerre."

I looked back as I turned the corner to go upstairs and she was still standing by my locker with her arms crossed and a puzzled expression on her face.

THE PASSING OF RALPH

"His feeble hart wide launched with loves cruell wound."

Edmund Spenser

"Who does that bitch think she is?" Teddy scowled at the tall, overdressed woman talking to the minister.

"She's the wedding director," I whispered. "It's her job to be a bitch."

"Well, if she keeps on at me, she's going to find out what a first-rate bastard is." He crossed his arms and sulked.

"Teddy, good grief, man, this is a church."

"I know it's a church. I'm not saying anything about God."

"Oh, good lord, Teddy-"

"He sure is. You'd better remember that."

He grinned and strolled down the aisle toward the altar leaving me standing in the vestibule of the First Presbyterian Church with Ralph's cousin Lloyd Dodge and the bridesmaids. Ralph, his betrothed, Susan, and the wedding director were standing down at the altar talking with the minister. Teddy stopped four or five pews from them and sat down. I turned to the group behind me.

I looked at the bridesmaids. They were two girls from Concord, friends of Susan's, and some Yankee girl who was Susan's roommate at UNC.

Susan, finishing her freshman year in college, was a year older than Ralph was. They'd met at a party during Christmas. Teddy and I had gotten caught trying to steal liquor from the locked cabinet at the home where the party was. Susan was a guest there. Anyway, Susan and Ralph started seeing each other regularly, Ralph going down to Chapel Hill first on the weekends, then later, during the week, too. Teddy and I knew they were serious, but then Ralph came to us and said he was getting married and wanted us to be ushers.

That was April and here it is May. They got the whole thing together in three weeks. My mom says it usually takes a lot longer to plan something like that. Teddy and I talked it over and decided that there must be a reason for the rush. We didn't say anything to Ralph, though.

"A penny for your thoughts," said the roommate. Like most Yankees, she talked a little through her nose. She was nice-looking, though, olive skin, dark eyes and black hair.

"A lire for yours."

"Oh, a wise guy, huh?" She turned away.

"Hey, I didn't mean anything by that. I've not met many Italian girls."

"I'm not Italian. I'm American. I was born in Trenton, New Jersey." She didn't turn around.

"Why couldn't you have been born in Eden?"

She looked over her shoulder at me. "Why do you say that?"

"Because then I could have met you sooner." I smiled.

She turned around. She tilted her head and considered me. Head tilting seems to be pretty popular among girls I've known.

"That's cute," she said. "Say, do you know if the cake cutting is here or some place else?"

"Here, I think. At the fellowship hall."

"Will there be anything to drink?" She raised her eyebrows.

"Sure. Lime punch or something."

She looked around, then stepped closer. "No, silly, I mean a real drink," she whispered.

"Oh. A real drink. Well." I stepped still closer to her and motioned for her to learn her ear near my lips. "My friend Teddy and I have three bottles of wine on ice in the trunk of his car. We're going to give a bottle to Ralph and Susan. That leaves two bottles, one for Teddy, one for me. You can share some of my bottle if you like."

"Is that Teddy?" She pointed down the aisle. Teddy was swaggering toward us, hands in pockets, tousled brown hair, and blue eyes. I looked at her looking at him and got the message.

"Yeah, that's him. He'll share his wine, too." I went to Teddy and stopped him. "The small dark-haired one wants your body," I said.

"Who? Anna?"

"Yeah. How'd you get her name?"

"I asked Susan. I've had my eye on her. So she thinks we can have a little fun, hey?"

"You've got it, ace."

"Well, I think she can get what she wants."

"No doubt." I shrugged. "Enjoy."

He put his arm around my shoulders. "Look, they're staying here tonight."

"Who?"

He shook his head at my stupidity. "The bridesmaids. Ralph's aunt and uncle down in Draper are putting them up. Ralph wants us to take them out after the cake cutting. So he and Susan can be alone." He waggled his eyebrows.

"As usual." I looked back at the other two girls still standing in the vestibule. "Who do I get?" I asked, peering at them. The vestibule was dark and they were in shadow.

About that time the wedding director called everyone to the front. They came out of the dark and I got a good look at them. There was a strawberry blonde with fabulous legs and a brunette, kind of pretty in an off-handed way. She reminded me a little bit of Jenny. I immediately rejected her.

I nudged Teddy. "I think I'll have strawberry."

He smiled. "An excellent choice. Ralph says she's dynamite with a short fuse. She was Susan's best friend in high school. She goes to East Carolina. Ralph says she's pretty wild."

"She's pretty. I'll have to see about the wild." I looked at the side of Teddy's face. He was grinning. He stopped suddenly. "One thing, though," he said taking his arm from my shoulders and looking at me, serious.

I smiled knowingly. "Yes, I have protection."

"No, not that." The same serious tone.

"What, then?"

He exhaled strongly. "Her name's Jenny."

I didn't say anything. I thought about Jenny Swan. Then about Paula. Then about Jenny again. I looked at the girl. She was laughing at something Ralph had said. Then she looked at me. The smile slipped from her face. After a few seconds she caught her self and began talking with Ralph and the other bridesmaids again.

"Charlie?" Teddy spoke, but I kept looking at the girl, even though she wouldn't return my look.

"Hmm?"

"Does it matter?"

"Hmm?"

"That her name's Jenny. Does it matter?"

I didn't answer.

"Is it okay?"

I didn't answer. He shook me and I looked at him soberly. "Yeah. It's okay."

We nodded somberly and joined the others up at the altar.

II

The rehearsal took about another thirty minutes. The wedding director yelled her head off. Reverend Whitsun, the retired minister from First Presbyterian who was performing the ceremony, was his usual placid self. His wife, my first grade teacher, sat in the front row and smiled at everything, just as she had when I was a first grader. Anna Verona, the roommate, winked at Teddy throughout the rehearsal. He kept grinning and the director kept yelling at him. Jenny looked at me three different times with a steady gaze that must have lasted at least thirty seconds each time. The first time she did it, it bothered me, but after that I didn't really react because I was watching Teddy and trying not to laugh. Still, I could feel her looking at me.

After we'd marched in for the fifteenth time and Reverend Whitsun had gone through the ceremony "with his fingers crossed" as he kept telling us, it was over. I'd walked out with Jenny on my arm several times, but she hadn't spoken and I hadn't been able to think of anything clever to say to open the conversation. The last time we walked out together, she tripped on the doorjamb at the front of the church and I caught her. She gave me that heavy-duty stare again. "I'm glad you're not Gort," I said.

"Who?" She narrowed her eyes.

"Gort," I continued placidly. "He's a character in this great sci-fi movie *The Day the Earth Stood Still*. He's a giant robot. He had this cover over his eyes. When it opened up he shot out disintegrating rays. As hard as you've been looking at me, I'd be all gone by now." I'd been holding her arm. She slipped away from me.

"You remind me of someone," she said. She looked out at the street.

"The old flame syndrome." I went around the side of the church toward the fellowship hall.

"What do you mean, 'the old flame syndrome'?" she called, coming behind me.

"Skip it." I kept walking.

She ran up and whirled me around, then kissed me. "Why'd you do that?" I asked, rubbing my mouth with the back of my hand.

"You said, 'skip it,' didn't you?" She noticed my hand. "You didn't like it?" She meant the kiss.

I dropped my hand and smiled wryly at her. "I liked it." A pause. "So, that dumb kissing game went around your junior high, too?"

"Um hmm. Eighth grade. I must have been kissed a hundred times. I used to say 'skip it' every chance I got." She wrinkled her nose.

"A hundred times. That's a lot of kisses. Didn't you worry about mono?" I smiled slyly.

She tossed her hair and took my arm. "I gargled a lot to kill germs," she said haughtily.

We both laughed. We walked to the fellowship hall. We went through the receiving line and shook hands with Ralph and Susan, all the parents, and a few other assorted relatives. We got some punch and cake and sat down on two of the little folding chairs lining the walls of the room. "Boy, Mr. and Mrs. Dodge look pretty tight-lipped," I said, watching them shake hands with people.

"Um hmm." She sipped her punch.

"Mr. and Mrs. Lily, too." Susan's parents.

"Oh, I guess putting on a wedding is a big strain," she said between bites of cake.

"Yeah. I bet it is," I was watching her to see if she gave anything away about Ralph and Susan. She kept her eyes on her plate, and I couldn't tell if she knew anything.

I thought of asking her point blank about Ralph and Susan, but someone caught my eye. It was Teddy. He was waving me over to the door. I excused myself and went over to him. "Listen," he whispered, "Anna and I are going for a ride out to the golf course. You and Jenny want to come?"

"Sure. Are we going to be able to do this openly, or do we have to 'disappear' in the next few minutes?"

He smiled. "Everything's taken care of. Lloyd's going to take Mary home."

"Who?"

"Mary. The other bridesmaid."

"Oh. Yeah."

"Ralph and Susan are going to suggest we all go somewhere together. Since six of us can't go in one car, Ralph will take his car and we four will go in mine."

I nodded. "Very good. Very nice. What happens then?" I asked facetiously.

"The golf course, amigo." He waggled his eyebrows again.

"Ralph and Susan?"

"They have many last minute details they want to discuss." He gave me a knowing look.

"I see." I gave him back the look. "When do we leave?"

"Now, if you're ready."

I grinned. "I was born ready."

III

We gave our dishes to the ladies in the kitchen. As we came out of the kitchen we saw Ralph and Susan taking leave of Reverend and Mrs. Whitsun, Ralph his usual imperturbable self, Susan clinging to him as if he might fly away. Ralph reached into his pocket and handed me his car keys. "Lay your 'present' on the front seat," he said, looking theatrically serious.

"Right."

"Jenny," said Susan, "you all need to be home by midnight." Very serious.

"Right," she said. I glanced at her. She squeezed my hand and whispered, "Just having fun."

"Right," I repeated.

"Charlie?" said Susan shyly.

"Yes?"

"I appreciate you and Teddy being in the wedding. Ralph and I are grateful."

"No problem. Glad to do it."

"Glad?" said Ralph in mock indignation.

"Just an expression, Ralph."

"Right," he said. We smiled and shook hands. Teddy came up then, and he and Ralph shook hands. Jenny shook Susan's hand, then Anna's. When she grabbed mine, I put a stop to her foolishness.

"Let's go." I pulled her toward the door. "Teddy, you all ready to go?"

"Right." He and Anna followed.

"Damn, what have I started?" I muttered. Jenny gave me a light punch on the arm. "Don't use bad language in church," she whispered.

"Sorry."

"You're a great one for one word sentences, aren't you?" she said as we crossed the street to Teddy's car.

"Yep."

"Gary Cooper." We stopped in the middle of the street to let a car pass in the other lane.

"What?" I held her against me as the car went by.

"Gary Cooper. The movie star. You know."

"Yeah, I know. What about him?"

She gave me a teacher look and we crossed the other lane. "He spoke in one word sentences. He was famous for it."

"Oh. Yeah."

"See? Gary Cooper." She patted my cheek as we leaned against Teddy's car. Teddy and Anna came up. He opened the trunk and handed me a bottle, cold and dripping. "Here's Ralph's wine," he said.

I held the bottle down by my leg. "Good lord, boy, watch that foolishness on a public street. You'll get us arrested. Where's Ralph's car?"

"Parked over by the church doors. We rode here with them," said Anna.

"Perfect," I said sarcastically.

"Gary Cooper."

I gave Jenny a mock frown. "Quiet, please. Teddy, pull over there." He was opening the passenger side door and letting Anna in. Jenny had walked around to get into the back seat on that side.

"It's dark, Charlie. Just trot over there and put the thing in Ralph's car. And don't forget to leave his keys on the front seat." Teddy closed the door, the girls in the car.

"What if some of those adults come out to their cars? How do I explain this to them?" I waved the bottle even as I stepped back into the street to turn and go.

"Aw, go on, Charlie, it'll be-" he was interrupted by squealing tires and roaring engine. Steve Castle's silver '55 Chevy slid around the corner of Spring and Bridge Streets, not a hundred feet away and hurtled toward me. I threw myself onto the trunk of Teddy's car. Steve screamed by only inches from our car going at least forty and accelerating. A police car slid into the intersection just as Steve passed and hurtled by almost as close to us. Teddy had reached across the trunk to grab me by the coat. I clutched the wine bottle.

"You okay?" he said as the police car went over the hill a couple of hundred feet away, lights flashing, siren screaming.

I lay on my back on the trunk of his car. I put the hand not clutching the wine bottle on my heart. "Yeah," I said, "it's still beating. I guess I'm not dead."

Teddy tousled my hair. "Hang on, hero. I'll get you across the road. It's too dangerous to let you walk." I looked in the back window of the car. Jenny was looking out, her fingers to her lips in the classic pose of the frightened woman.

"Fay Wray," I said through the glass.

She stared a second, then caught the joke. She smiled. "Touché."

"Ah, francais. - Parlez vous?"

"Nein. Ich spreche deutsche."

"No kidding. German?" I rolled off the car and crawled into the back seat with her as Teddy held open the door. Anna pulled back the front seat to let me in.

"Not many schools offer German," Jenny said, cuddling against me. "I was lucky."

"Truly."

"Back to Gary Cooper."

"You know," I said, leaning back in the seat, "I'd like to learn some German."

"I'll teach you some," Jenny said, leaning back with me.

"Good." I pulled her close so that our faces were only an inch apart. "And I'll teach you some French."

She smiled, blurry. "Humphrey Bogart," she murmured.

I didn't let her say anything else.

IV

"And then Old Man Delight said, 'I'm gonna get my shotgun and blow your head off.' "

"God, Teddy, what did you do then?" Anna's eyes were wide in the moonlight.

"He turned to Mr. Delight and said, 'You haven't got the guts,' " I said. I took another drink from the bottle of champagne, which was about two-thirds empty. I followed that with a swig of beer.

"What were *you* doing during all this?" Jenny asked. She took the champagne and chugged down a goodly portion, then motioned for the beer. She swallowed some and looked steadily at me.

I returned her look. "I stayed in the car out of the direct line of fire."

"Were you afraid?" She touched me with her hand.

"Hell, yes. You'd have to be crazy, deaf, dumb, and blind not to be. Delight was the meanest man I've ever met."

"Anna rubbed her face against Teddy's chest, then sat up. "Well, tell us," she said, unbuttoning his shirt, "what happened?"

Teddy smiled at me. "Talks just like a Yankee, don't she, Charlie? Right through her adenoids."

"I don't have any adenoids." She drew herself up haughtily. "The doctor took them out when I was seven."

"Then you talk through where your adenoids used to be." Teddy drained the last of the champagne from his bottle. "Well, that's that," he said, holding it up in the moonlight.

He stood up. We were sitting on the fifteenth tee at Meadow Greens Country Club. It was a par three. You had to hit across a big pond to the elevated green. Teddy threw his bottle at the pond about twenty yards away. It landed with a thump and bounced into the water. We could see it bobbing in the moonlight.

"You about ready, Charlie boy?" He was pretty tight. We all were. We'd been drinking champagne chased by beer the girls had bought.

"Just about. We've got a couple of drinks left. You want any more, Jenny?" I held out the bottle.

She took it and drained the rest. "Not now." She handed me the bottle and leaned over and bit me on the throat. I eased away from her and stood. I drained the rest of the beer we'd been drinking. I wasn't woozy, just very mellow.

Anna held her hand up to the beer as I let it down. "Me some," she slurred. I handed her the empty can and she drained the few drops. She got to her feet and dropped the can. She stepped out of her shoes and started down the hill at a dogtrot. "Going swimming," she called. "In the nude. Anybody want to come, too?"

"Hey, come back here," I called. "Stop her, Teddy. The water's deep right to the edge of that pond." Jenny stood and leaned on my shoulder.

Teddy stared numbly for a few moments. Anna reached the edge of the pond. She was wiggling out of her pantyhose, then she was in the water, her hose tangled about her feet. I sprinted down the hill toward the lake. She came up once, spluttering just as I got to the edge. I pulled off my shoes and jumped in after her. I got my arms around her legs and pulled her to me. She kicked and accidentally kneed me in the groin, so I turned her loose. I caught at her foot as she sank by me. By then Teddy was in the water. Jenny was there, too, and got Anna's head up. The three of us managed to get her out onto the bank. She'd swallowed some water, but not much. In a few moments she was sitting up, coughing, but reassuring us she was okay. Teddy pulled her hose off. Then he wrapped her up tightly in his arms.

"Let's go down to the river," he said suddenly, sitting up. We helped the girls to their feet. We struggled back up the hill. At the top Anna remembered her hose.

"Forget them," I said. "Let some golfer find them tomorrow and go crazy trying to figure out where they came from."

We laughed. Jenny picked up the beer cans and our wine bottle. She put them in a trashcan over at the edge of the tee. Then she picked up a blanket and handed it to Teddy. The other she held out to me. "Can we build a fire down at the river?" she asked.

"Sure. Why?"

She smiled and I thought she was going to call me Gary Cooper again. "I'm going to strip and dry my clothes as best I can," she said. "How about you?" She winked.

"There's only one blanket for both of us," I said flatly.

She stepped close. "Then it works out well that I'm female and you're male, doesn't it?"

I looked over to Teddy and Anna, but they were kissing like they were on fire. I thought of Paula. And Jenny Swan. "You won't mind?" I asked stupidly.

She kissed me and put my fears to rest.

V

"That's a sad story." She snuggled closer.

"Yeah, it is." I kissed her neck. Her skin was a funny combination of pond water and perfume. We sat leaning against the big rock. A strong fire dried our clothes, draped on sapling branches Teddy and I'd cut down with the old hunting knife Ralph had given me. We'd arranged them around the fire. The fire crackled. A fish jumped. We could sometimes hear the murmur of Teddy's and Anna's voices as they lay wrapped in the other blanket on the far side of the fire.

"You and Teddy and Ralph have had some adventures, haven't you?" Jenny murmured, leaning against me.

"Yeah, we've had some wild times." I kissed the side of her face.

"Ralph used to talk a lot about you three. He made it sound like the Three Musketeers." She rubbed the inside of my leg.

"Three Stooges is more like it," I mumbled, rubbing my face in her hair.

"Oh, Charlie." She fondled me. I rubbed her breast and we went under the blanket again.

After a while we lay still. The fire crackled as a piece of wood slipped. We could hear the river rushing along and frogs making sounds. Another fish jumped. Then we heard Teddy and Anna, and began talking so as not to hear them. "Charlie?" Jenny whispered.

"Hmm?"

"Do you come down here often?"

"Whenever I want to fish." A big one jumped about midstream.

"Charlie?"

"Hmm?"

"Have you ever been in love?" She traced her fingers on my chest.

 "Yeah."

"How did it turn out?"

I turned and lay on my back. "Badly."

She lay her leg over my groin. What did you do to get over it?"

"I don't know." I slid more tightly against her. "I cried."

"You did?" She flipped the covers back so that our heads were exposed. She looked at me in the firelight. "You cried?"

"Yeah, I did," I said, looking straight at her.

"Oh." She lay her head on my chest. "What else did you do?"

"I read books. I read *Hans Brinker*. And some stories by Ernest Hemingway about a guy named Nick. And a play by a guy name Congreve called *The Way of the World*. And *Kings and Things*."

"What's that?"

"It's a book my grandmother gave me. It's about English history. It's written for little kids. I've liked it a lot, every since I was about eight or nine."

"What else did you do?"

"Well, Teddy and Ralph took me out with them. They got me to doing things again. They're real friends, I guess."

"Yeah." She kissed me on the chin. "Now, I guess, you've only got Teddy." She paused. "In a manner of speaking."

"Yeah. I guess so."

"Charlie?"

"Hmm?"

"What do you want to be?"

I sighed. "Happy. Like I am now."

She kissed me. "No, I mean, what do you want to do with your life?"

"I don't know. I truly don't."

"Ralph says you write poetry."

I grunted. "Ralph says a lot of things."

"Charlie?"

"Hmm?"

"Do you think I'm pretty?" Her hand clutched one of mine.

"God, yes." Her hand relaxed. "I was just wondering what someone who looks like you was doing here with me."

She kissed me again. "Our clothes will be dry in a little while. Let's just relax until they are." She pulled the blanket back over our heads.

We lay listening to the crickets, the frogs, and the fish. And the river slid by like time, faster than we realized.

WHAT SOME SAY ABOUT EDEN

"Here's looking at you, kid."

Humphrey Bogart

"Two-oh-four, Charlie Beagle." The intercom blared in the hall of the dormitory.

"Two-oh-four, Charlie Beagle."

"All page, Charlie Beagle."

I stuck my head out into the hall and answered sleepily, "Yeah?"

"You got a phone call, line two," the intercom droned.

"Thank you."

"No charge." The buzzing voice was silent.

I stumbled down the hall to the telephones. I picked up line one and spoke to the dial tone. Then I realized my mistake and switched to line two.

"Hello?"

A vaguely familiar female voice said softly, "Charlie?"

"Yeah."

"What time will you be home?"

"What?"

"What time will you be coming home, today?"

"My god, who is this?"

"Kathleen. Your sister."

"Kathleen. Kathleen," my voice rose in anger, "what the hell are you doing calling me at eight-thirty? I only got to bed at two this morning."

"Hello?" A new, eminently familiar voice came on the line.

"Well, who's that?"

"It's me. Your daddy. I told Kathleen to call you. I thought I heard you use foul language to her."

"It's too early to think." I couldn't believe I was standing in my underwear in a cold hallway at eight-thirty in the morning chatting with my father about profanity.

"Listen here, boy," he said in his most dominant voice, "I want you to come home as soon as you can get dressed."

I shivered. Someone had left the French doors that led to the balcony at the end of the hall next to where I was standing ajar, and a cool autumn breeze was blowing through giving me a chill designed to bring on pneumonia. "Why?" I asked crabbily.

"Because your Aunt Doris and Uncle Fred Barlow are coming in from California and they want to see you."

Sure they did. They'd seen me twice in fifteen years. The last time they'd seen me, I'd been eleven, and we'd had a good family talk for maybe forty-five seconds. "I can't come right away."

"Come early." His master's voice.

"What time is 'early'?"

"About one this afternoon."

I had a date to eat lunch with Barbara Snow at twelve. Then we were going to play tennis. Then, maybe go to her room. "No way I can, Dad. I've got classes until four." It was easier than arguing with him over some girl.

"Well, then, you can go with your mother and me tonight."

"Where are y'all going?" I didn't really want to know.

"Out to eat with Fred and Doris. You can visit with them that way." There was no way out. I made a mental note never to be definite about coming home for the weekend again.

"All right. But I might have to slip away early."

"We'll see about that. We'll be expecting you about four-thirty."

"More like five o'clock. I'll see you then, Dad."

"See you this evening, son."

"Yes sir. Goodbye."

"Goodbye."

I hung up. The breeze gusted and swung one of the French doors open, hitting me in the heel and freezing me at the same time. I hopped shivering down the hall muttering curses at the world in general and at Fred and Doris Barlow in particular.

II

I got to Eden about five-thirty. Before I went home, I stopped at a phone booth and called Teddy's house. His mom said he wasn't home from Raleigh yet, but that she expected him any time. She told me she'd tell him to call me. "You'll be at home, Charlie?"

"Yes ma'am." I hoped so. At least Kathleen probably would be, and he'd know where to look for me.

When I walked in the back door my mother was in a flutter. "Hurry, Charlie. Go to your room and get out of those jeans. Put on your nice gray pants and a shirt and tie. You can borrow one of your father's sport coats if all yours are at school."

"Mother, I'm fine as I am." I didn't want to dress up for people I could barely remember.

"Now, Charlie, don't be difficult. Your father's going to be upset enough with you for being so late."

"Am I late?" I asked innocently.

"Son, it's ten of six and we're supposed to meet Fred and Doris at the Meadow Greens Steak House at six. Now hurry."

I strolled to my room and closed the door. As I fished in the closet for a shirt and tie, I heard my father come in from outside. He and Mother discussed for a bit whether or not he should yell at me. I pulled out a blue shirt and a red and blue striped tie. I fumbled in the floor of my closet until I found a pair of loafers that didn't look too beaten up. I took off my tennis shoes. I put on some dark socks and slipped the loafers on. There was something in the toe of one of them, and while I fingered around in it trying to get whatever it was out, my father opened the door and stuck his head into my room. "You're awfully late, boy," he said in his deepest voice.

"I got tied up." I kept fooling with the shoe and avoided looking at him.

"What was her name?"

"Barbara." I pulled a piece of old chewing gum from the shoe. "How in the world did that get in there?"

"What is it?" He stepped into the room and peered at the gum.

"A piece of gum."

"Chewing gum?"

"Yeah."

"You about ready?" he asked, surprisingly friendly.

"In a minute."

"Well, hurry it up. We're late now." The door clapped shut and he was gone. I tossed the gum at the garbage can in the far corner.

I slid off my pullover shirt and put the blue button-up on slowly. I stood and slipped my foot into my shoe. I scooped the tie from the bed and started for the door, then remembered that I didn't have a jacket. I rummaged in the closet and found my old navy blazer. It didn't look too bad, so I put it on and draped the tie around my neck.

I went down the hall past the den, turned right and cut through the dining room, then into the kitchen and out the back door. Kathleen was at the door. "Hurry, Charlie," she said.

"If Teddy calls, tell him where they're holding me."

She wrinkled her nose at me. "Oh, you think you're so cute. I wish I could go."

"Take my place." Dad blew the horn.

"Have fun," she called as I went to the car.

"Now who's being cute?" I called back at her. I opened the back door on the passenger's side and got in.

"Well, we're late," said my father. He backed out of the driveway and we headed down the hill into Eden.

III

As we drove to the Meadow Greens Steak House, my dad chewed me out for wearing jeans. I listened calmly as I tried to see myself in the rearview mirror so that I could tie my necktie. I got it tied, flipped my shirt collar down and straightened my jacket. As we drove through downtown Eden, I checked the clock on the Southern National Bank building. It said six-fifteen. My dad would be pissed off at me all weekend for making him late. No use asking him for money this weekend, I decided. I figured I'd go by and see if my grandmother could spare a few bucks. Maybe I could rake leaves or mow her yard or something. I sat back and looked at all the new buildings going up along King's Highway.

"Pretty soon, you won't know Eden," my mother said, looking around at me. "This new construction is changing the town."

"Guess so." I looked out my window at a new bank going up on my left.

"Eden's coming alive," my dad said, tapping a cigarette on the ashtray as he slowed down for the traffic signal at the intersection of King's Highway and N.C. 14.

"Not for me," I said.

The car turned left on 14, then left again into the shopping center. We eased to a stop in a parking place near the steak house. I dragged a couple of steps behind my folks as we crossed the parking lot.

My father flipped away his cigarette butt and turned to me. "I guess you're too good for Eden now that you're a college boy."

"No. No, that's not true," I said.

My mother patted his arm. "Don't be so hard on the boy, Charles."

My father grunted and walked on, opened the door to the steak house, and motioned Mother in. I stopped and watched. When I finally got myself into the restaurant, they'd already gone into the dining area. I asked the hostess about them. She said that I was to go right in. I turned and started into the restaurant, but the bar caught my eye and I decided it was worth at least a look. I stepped in. It was pretty dark except for a couple of beer signs. I went to the bar. "Let me have a draft, please," I said to the bartender.

"He looked hard at me in the gloom. "You got I.D.?"

I showed him my draft card. After he'd looked at it and given it back to me, I stood looking at it for a minute, wondering how in hell I'd got so old so fast. The beer slid into my view.

"There you go. A draft for the man with a draft card." I looked up. He was smiling. I smiled back. It was a good joke.

I sipped the beer and checked out the room. There was a Schlitz clock on the wall. There was a Pabst lamp on a plastic chain suspended over the far end of the bar. At the other end, an illuminated replica of the Anheuser-Busch wagon stood next to the cash register. It was the kind of place where a guy who'd grown up watching beer commercials could feel at home.

I came to myself and took a couple of long pulls at the beer. I figured I'd better hustle before my father came looking for me. I took a deep breath and chugged the rest down. I got that pleasant warm feeling in my stomach and felt it start climbing toward my face. I looked for the bartender. He was at the far end of the bar putting bottles of beer into a cooler. "Hey, how much for the draft?" I called softly.

"Two years, last I heard." He kept breaking open six packs and sticking them into the cooler.

One joke comedian, I thought. "No, I meant for the beer."

"Forty cents."

I took two quarters out. I clicked them and he looked up. I laid them on the bar, pointed at them, and he nodded. I went outside and bought a pack of peppermint gum from the cashier. I put two sticks into my mouth and went in to find my folks.

They were all the way across the room. I threaded my way through the other diners to them. When I got to their table I stood there with my hands in the pockets of my jeans.

"Well, this must be Charlie," said the woman, who must be Doris.

"Looks like Charles, don't he?" said the man, who must be Fred.

"We were getting worried," my mother said, watching my gum.

"I ran into a friend." I shrugged.

"Where'd you run into him?" My father asked sarcastically.

"In the bar." I popped the gum.

"Charlie, honey," my mother leaned over and tugged my sleeve, "take that gum out of your mouth. It makes you hard to understand."

I took the gum out and put it into the ashtray. My father scowled and moved his cigarette. "Scoot over, Charles," said my mother. "Let's make room for Charlie."

They were in one of those big, horseshoe-shaped booths. My dad slid over, forcing everyone else to. I sat down at the end of the group. I looked at everybody pleasantly. They were all looking at me expectantly. They kept looking at me. I looked across the room. There was a guy in his forties with a girl in her twenties. He had his arm around her and was tickling her on the chin. It reminded me of a movie.

"Did y'all ever see *Of Human Bondage*?" I said, to nobody in particular. "It's about this guy named Phillip. He falls in love with this real b-witch played by Bette Davis. Anyway, she treats him like dirt all the time, and he takes it 'cause he loves her. She's fooling around with this other, older married guy, only he, Leslie Howard that is, doesn't know it. Anyway, they have a bunch of scenes of the older guy acting like *that* with Bette Davis-" I pointed at the couple and they all looked "-then one rainy night Bette shows up at Leslie Howard's apartment and she's knocked up- I mean pregnant- so he takes her in. Meanwhile, during the time when Bette was doing all this, old Leslie was fooling around with this really nice woman-I can't remember her name-and when Bette shows up Leslie drops *her* like a hot potato so he can take care of Bette. Then, after Bette has the kid by this other guy, she dumps on old Leslie again and again until she burns herself out and dies. That couple over there reminded me of that movie. It's from a novel by Somerset Maugham, an English writer. I'm gonna read that book over Christmas; it's been preying on my mind. Do you all ever think stuff like that just from seeing something or someone?"

They were all looking at me as if I had two heads, except for my mother, who was squinting at the couple. "Charles," she said, tugging Dad's sleeve, I believe that's Mary Lord, Dr. Lord's daughter. I don't know the man, though." She looked at him for confirmation.

He nodded. "That's her. The man's John Fireman. Owns Fireman's Jewelry. He and his wife divorced last year." He shook his head disapprovingly.

"I remember John Fireman," said Doris, looking hard at the couple. "We were at Leaksville High together. He was a year younger than me."

"Oh, to hell with it." I stood up.

"What do you mean, coming out with something like that?" My father rasped. "Apologize right now."

I stood there looking at them, thinking of all the things I could say. "I'm sorry," I said, insincerely.

My father motioned at the seat. "Sit back down."

I didn't move.

"Sit back down, boy." My father glared. The waitress came up with a tray and began handing salads to everyone.

"Sit down and order, Charlie." Mother glanced at me, then at Doris and Fred.

"I'll be back. I have to be excused." I walked away, weaving around the tables. When I got to the lobby, I asked the cashier where the restrooms were. She pointed to a sign about five feet away hanging over a hallway next to the entrance. I went into the little hall, then into the restroom, right through a door marked "Gentlemen."

After I used the bathroom, I washed my hands. The faucet was one of those kinds that won't stay turned on, so I had to hold the tap on with one hand while I stuck the other under, then use the clean hand to hold the dirty tap so that I could wet the other. It seemed to me that having to handle the taps defeated the purpose of washing my hands. They didn't have paper towels, just one of those blower machines, so I held my hands out in front of me and shook them. You get the same effect. While I shook my hands, I eyed myself in the mirror. I didn't look too bad, except that my image was getting more distorted by the second because I was slinging water on the mirror. My hair was a little mussed, so I took my fingers and straightened my part.

I went out of the restroom and into the lobby again. The bar tempted me, so I stuck my head in through the beads that they had hanging in the doorway. Teddy Hatter was standing at the bar.

IV

"Aw, I was telling them about this movie I saw, *Of Human Bondage*, and they started talking about whose daughter the girl was and that one of them had gone to school with the man and a whole bunch of crap that I didn't want to hear. It's like everything I said just went slam over their heads."

"Maybe it did, Charlie." Teddy strummed a couple of chords on his guitar. "Hand me a beer."

I reached down and pulled the string with the beer tied to it out of the river. I handed one across the fire to Teddy. As he opened it, I reached behind me and threw a couple of more pieces of wood on the fire. I picked up my own beer, killed the last of it, and stuck the empty bottle into the paper sack that held the other empties. "You feel anything yet?" I asked.

"Nope. Must be my sixth or seventh, counting the one I had in the bar before you walked in. Don't really feel it." Teddy tossed his empty to me and I put it in the sack.

"Must be the weather," I said.

"It is sorta cool, isn't it?"

"Yeah, it is." I drew my blazer around me more tightly. "I'm glad we made the fire."

"Me, too." He smiled, rather to himself. "Reminds me of that night with Anna Verona and Jenny Malone."

I smiled in turn, then looked at the river and remembered. "Me, too," I said absently.

A fish set my reel singing so I grabbed my rod and pulled back sharply to set the hook. I reeled it in. It was a fair sized catfish. In the firelight I could see that it was a speckled channel cat. I worked the hook from its mouth and let it slip back into the water. "That's not too common a fish here in the Dan River," I said, more to myself than to Teddy.

"Really?" Teddy idly strummed chords.

"Nope. Mostly blue cats in the Dan River. That was a channel cat. They're mostly Smith River fish. Daddy says that's because channel cats like a sandy bottom better. Smith's bottom is sandier."

Teddy laid his guitar in its case. "What do you reckon your dad will do when you go home, Charlie?" he asked quietly.

"Raise hell awhile. Then Mother will calm him down and he'll go off growling. Then she'll start in on me with that soft accusing way of hers and make me feel worse than hell for skipping out on the dinner and being rude to my great aunt and uncle." I'd been putting another shrimp on my hook. I drew back the rod and flipped line out into the river. I watched the end of the rod and saw the current drag the line downstream until it went taut. It bobbed up and down gently as the river tugged at it. I returned my attention to Teddy. He was toying with his guitar again. I leaned back on my elbows. "I went down to the river/ To watch the fish swim by," I sang.

"What song is that?" Teddy asked.

" ' Long Gone Lonesome Blues.' It's by Hank Williams."

"Yeah. I think I've heard it." He began strumming the chords on his guitar.

"You know, Teddy, I'm really glad you had this fishing rod in your car's trunk."

"You really like to fish, don't you, Charlie?"

"Yeah." I sat up and rested my chin on my arms, which were resting on my drawn up knees.

Teddy put his guitar away. He leaned back on his elbows and looked across the fire at me. "So. How's UNC since the last rehearsal?"

"Okay. My classes aren't bad. Wish I had more time for the band. I'm really digging journalism. I think I may major in that."

"How's N. C. State? I need to get over to Raleigh, but you're always in Chapel Hill, so—" I watched the tip of my rod jiggle.

"I don't like it. It's not what I want. I should play guitar less and study more, but I don't see that happening. I think I'll transfer to UNC with you, Mick—and Jay Brent, maybe—so we can work on the band more. I'd like to rehearse more, play more shows, make a demo tape...." He looked off at the river, lost in thought.

"UNC may not be what you want, either—and Jay's not a maybe, he's a definite for the band." I looked askance at him and smiled.

He grinned. "Yeah."

I rolled over onto my side. Teddy got up and walked around behind me. He got some wood and brought it around and put it on the fire. He returned to his side of the fire. "You know something I hate, Charlie?" he said suddenly.

"What?"

"Not being able to explain anything to anybody."

"What's 'anything'?"

"Diana. The riot. Miss Leila. All that stuff."

"Oh." I shifted to relieve my arm of my weight.

"What do you think?" Teddy asked.

I shrugged. "It doesn't really bother me."

"It doesn't?" He sat up and peered across the fire at me."

"Nope." I sat up and looked at him. "I can't explain why. It's like-like I understand it all. Raoul Lamb. Jenny Swan. Jenny Malone. Paula. All of it. I just understand it."

"What do you mean, you 'understand it'?"

I shrugged. "Hell, I don't know. I just do. It doesn't bother me." I hugged my knees and watched the river. "You know what does bother me?"

Teddy stood and pulled up the beer string. He took two off and let the last one fall back in the river with a splash. "Hey, you'll scare the fish," I said.

"Sorry." He smiled and handed me one of the beers. I sat and looked at it, thoughtful. He sat down and opened his beer and took a long pull at it. "I think these just kicked in," he said, chuckling and steadying himself with his hand. "You were about to say what bothered you."

I opened my beer. I took a drink, then put the beer between my knees and stared at the river. Finally I nodded at the river. "That bothers me."

"The river?" I looked at him across the fire. He was looking at me as if I'd just said the dumbest thing in the world. He put his hand up to his chin and stroked it like an old man.

"You want to be an old man, don't you, Teddy?" I said.

"That's what I'm living for." He looked out over the river. "When you're an old man, you don't have to do anything you don't want to. And you don't have to play all kinds of stupid games with girls. Or with anybody else, for that matter." He took another long drink of beer. "Why does the river bother you?"

"Because it goes on and on. It never changes. It flows, no matter what. Like Miss Leila died, and Ralph got married, and we graduated and went off to college. And we'll get married and grow old and die. And the river will get all that. And it'll just keep going. Like the song."

"Old Man Ribber/Dat Old Man Ribber," Teddy sang in a bad imitation of Paul Robeson. I didn't laugh, so he rolled onto his side and dangled his beer in his hand.

I lay back, balanced my beer on my stomach, and put my hands behind my head. I looked up at the sky. The blanket was a little scratchy on the backs of my hands, and I thought about strawberry-haired Jenny and that night four months before. To stop thinking about her, I looked up at the sky. The stars were very clear. They were really distant. I tried to think of something to tell Teddy about my feeling about the river. Then I saw a falling star. "Go and catch a falling star," I said in a low voice.

"What's that?" Teddy said.

"I said, 'Go and catch a falling star.' It's from a poem by John Donne."

He put his beer on the ground beside him. "I know him. He wrote that 'Death Be Not Proud.' He held up his beer toward the river, as if in toast. " 'Death, thou shalt die.' That's some line." I didn't respond. Teddy lay back as I was lying and looked at the sky. "Wonder what they're doing on Mars tonight?"

"Probably lying on the bank of one of the canals and wondering what they're doing on Earth tonight." I raised my head enough to take a drink of my beer.

"Good answer." He took a drink himself. "Well?"

"Well, what?"

"What about the river?"

"I'll figure it out someday." I sighed.

"What if you never figure it out?"

"Good question." I picked up my beer and sat up. I took a long drink. I set down the bottle and checked my line. The bait was gone. I put another piece of shrimp on and cast my line back into the river. I reached behind me and got more wood and put it on the fire. "It'll come to me one day." I leaned back on my elbows and watched the river. It was calm as it glistened in the firelight. I jumped up and walked to the edge of the water. I knelt down and looked at the river. It was moving swiftly, silently. I put my hand in the water. It was cold. I brought my hand to my face and touched my cheek. "Ol' Man River," I murmured.

"Ol' Man River, Dat Ol' Man River/ He don't say nothing, he just keeps rolling…" Teddy sang, very sincere.

I turned and grinned at him. "Nice voice."

"Thank you, sir, thank you." He bowed awkwardly, sitting up.

"I think sometimes we don't know how important we are, Teddy," I said, looking at the river.

"You and me?" He gestured at me, then himself.

"Anybody."

"Oh." He took a sip of his beer.

"We spend all of our time on what we do rather than what we are." I started to get excited. I could feel that same feeling come over me, the one I'd had talking to Mr. Newley about his statue and to Jenny about her and me. I hadn't had the feeling for a long time, but here it was back again. Just like when I was talking about *Of Human Bondage*.

"Hmm," Teddy said. He yawned.

"The river is what it is," I said. "It knows somehow that that's all it has to be. It doesn't have to *do* anything. When I was riding down to the steak house tonight, I was looking at all the new stuff they're building along King's Highway. It got me to thinking about how we've always got to be doing something. Humans, I mean. That's what makes us build stuff all the time. And have governments. And all that." I paused and drank the rest of my beer in greedy swallows.

"Like funerals," Teddy said flatly.

I wiped my hand across my mouth. "That's right. Like funerals. We can't even let death just be. We have to do something."

"I think I know why." Teddy got up and came down to the water. He put his hand into the river and brushed himself on each cheek with water. "It's because we're scared." He looked at me. In the dim light we nodded at each other.

"I wish Ralph were here," I said softly.

"Me, too." A pause. "Charlie?" he asked softly.

"Yeah?"

"Did you feel funny today when you came home?"

"Yeah. Like a stranger."

"No, not quite a stranger. Just strange."

"Okay. Just strange." I reached my hand back into the water. I brought it out and looked at it. In the firelight it glistened. "Some say you aren't really baptized until you've been dunked in running water." I looked at my fishing rod. Nothing but the current.

My great-grandmother believed that," Teddy said. "Primitive Baptist." He put his hand into the water again. "Let's swim the river," he said, looking at it.

"Why?"

"Call it a gesture." He smiled at me.

I shook my head, grinning. "I'd call it crazy."

"Let's do it."

"Okay." I reeled in my line. I laid the rod up by the fire. Teddy was already pulling off his clothes. I did the same. "Underwear?" I asked. He paused a moment, then nodded his head.

Stripped, I went back to the water's edge and stood beside him. "Can we dive?" he asked.

"Better not," I said. "Not in the dark, anyway." We stepped into the edge of the river. The water felt really cold. We waded out until up to our waists.

"Squat down," said Teddy. "It'll warm you up." We squatted. I looked over at Teddy. I could just make out the shape of his head above the water. "Let's go," he said.

I pushed off with my feet and started swimming. The current was stronger than it looked, and took us down stream about twenty feet. As we waded out on the other side, I glanced back at the fire, now upstream from us. "You okay?" I asked Teddy. I shook myself.

"Great."

A car came over the hill and its lights shone down right into Teddy's face. He was smiling. We walked up the bank toward the fire on the other side. The bank was sandy and broad. "This is a good place," I said. "Let's come here from now on."

"Why?"

I shrugged in the dark. "Call it a gesture." I put my hand on his shoulder. He jumped, startled. "What?" he asked.

I shrugged. "Nothing. Call it a gesture."

He laughed. "Good old Charlie." He put his arm around my shoulder. "You ready to swim back?"

"Yeah." We waded in and swam back. We dried ourselves on the blankets and put our clothes on. I got my fishing rod. We put the fire out. Just before we went up the hill, I looked back across the river. Another car's headlights flashed a beacon, then disappeared. I thought of Ralph. And Paula. And Jenny Swan. Behind me Teddy sneezed. "Let's go," he said.

"Okay." I walked up the hill behind him. When I got to the top, I looked back down at the big rock and the river. I couldn't see either. We threw the sack with empty beer cans into the car. We put the wet blankets and the fishing rod in the trunk. Teddy laid his guitar in the back seat. We got into the car and eased slowly away.

"You know," Teddy said, snapping on the radio, "that river's not very wide."

I looked at him. "It's wide enough." The radio began to play "Get Together" by the Youngbloods. I changed the station. "Instant Karma" by John Lennon came on:

"And we all shine on/Like the moon and the stars and the sun...."

"That seems fitting," Teddy said. He turned up the volume and gunned the engine. We took off, going somewhere else, leaving all that behind.

The End

Also by Jim Booth

The New Southern Gentleman

Completeness of the Soul: The Life and Opinions of Jay Breeze, Rock Star

The Wonderful Land of Eden